Dedicated to Mojo.

For her constant love and support.

CONTENTS

Chapter One
THE GIFT   1

Chapter Two
HAVISHAM HALL   8

Chapter Three
THE DREAM STREAMER   19

Chapter Four
ENTER THE CIRCLE   32

Chapter Five
SAMUEL BARBER   47

Chapter Six
GOIN UNDERGROUND   55

Chapter Seven
HYSTERIA AT HAVISHAM HALL   67

Chapter Eight
IN YOUR DREAMS   77

Chapter Nine
SIBLING RIVALRY   90

Chapter Ten
THE HUB   97

Chapter Eleven
THE CASE BEGINS   111

Chapter Twelve
PHOENIX RISING   116

Chapter Thirteen
PARK FIGHT   124

Chapter Fourteen
THE INFIRMARY   136

Chapter Fifteen
ZIVA, WARRIOR PRINCESS   143

Chapter Sixteen
SO FAR SO BAD   151

Chapter Seventeen
THE HOLOCITE SCROLLS   158

Chapter Eighteen
WAY DOWN IN THE HOLE   175

Chapter Nineteen
NIGHTMARES ON THE MOVE   182

Chapter Twenty
THE TEMPORAL CHAMBER   200

Chapter Twenty One
CLOSE SHAVE   219

Chapter Twenty Two
CHAOS IN THE CAVES   227

Chapter Twenty Three
WEATHER THE STORM   241

Chapter Twenty Four
NIGHTMARES ON APPLEGATE STREET   244

Chapter Twenty Five
GREAT EXPECTATIONS   261

Chapter One

THE GIFT

P oor Robbie Havisham never had it easy. He was pale and sickly and he had never been tall or particularly attractive. He was best described by a word that could mean good or bad. Different. Although he was eight years old, Robbie couldn't remember a single day that he didn't feel this way. He had jet-black hair that he blew out of his eyes when he got nervous, which people mistook for arrogance, and he was quiet and clever, which people mistook for self-assurance. People just didn't get him. In fact, at times, Robbie felt like his entire life was just one big problem, or at least an unbearable series of little ones.

The truth is Robbie's real problems started with headaches. Headaches that lasted for hours at a time and were especially bad at night, he tossed and turned in his bed trying to shake them free, but they just wouldn't leave. He believed he was going mad, or as his sister Lucy said "psycho." Lucy was two years older than her brother and she never let him forget it.

Robbie thought the headaches meant that he was sick, but his dad wouldn't hear of it, his dad knew exactly what was wrong with Robbie, and one Friday afternoon he summoned him to the study of their apartment to discuss it.

"Rob, Rob. Come here!" Peter Havisham sat at his desk, which as usual was covered in stacks of scientific notes, illustrations, and other documents that made no sense to anyone but him. He was a tall and skinny man with dirty brown hair who had partaken in lots of mental exercise, but nothing physical, which meant he was so pale that he had something called "the Havisham glow." Peter didn't mind any of the stupid nicknames that he got stuck with along the way, but it was different when it came to his family, family was sacred. Peter began taking out handfuls of books from the compartments in his desk. When Robbie entered he could see his father hunched over them. One stood out from the rest, it was a large leather bound edition with the words Havisham Family Tree written on it. "See this book?" Peter asked without looking up. Robbie nodded, making his way to the desk. "It's the most important book we own." Robbie looked down at the pages that were old and warped and full of crudely glued photographs. "It tells us who we are, who went before us. Look, that's your great great granddad," said Peter pointing to a photo of a man with an intense gaze, piercing eyes and a wide frazzled moustache, he looked serious, mean. "That's his wife, Margaret." Peter gestured to a woman who had a face like a disgruntled bulldog. The thought had occurred to Robbie that his dad was acting weird, weirder than usual that is, and wondered what exactly he was doing looking at a book full of old crazy people.

Peter flicked to the front of the book, looked at Robbie, and took a deep breath, as if he was either going to say something really important or explode. "This is the most important thing I'll ever tell you Rob. I'm telling you this because I think you're old enough to understand what it means. How amazing it is." He had Robbie's full attention. Peter pointed to a smartly dressed and well-manicured man with slicked back hair. "This is Jeremiah Havisham, the one who discovered our great gift." "Gift?" "Jeremiah was a scientist," said Peter "an extraordinary one. Here in London he began to research our family bloodline. He discovered that the Havisham name is incredibly important." "Why?" "Because of our special gene." "What do you mean special gene?" "A genius gene." "Genius gene?" blurted Robbie at how silly it sounded. "Exactly. Jeremiah, your granddad, myself, and now you and Lucy carry this gene."

Peter moved from behind his desk and knelt down beside Robbie at the opposite side. "Listen closely son, this gene, this gift, means we're very intelligent, more intelligent than others maybe, but it means a lot more than this. It means that we've inherited special, well, abilities." Robbie looked bemused. "Like, powers?" "More like side effects" said Peter somewhat grimly. "It means that if we use this gift properly we can change things, for the better. It's a gift that only Havishams possess." Just as the words left Peter's mouth his expression changed, as if he had just remembered something awful. "People are afraid of things they can't understand Rob, they're afraid of things that are different. But we can never use our abilities against them. As much as people push us around we can never let them know about this." "But, I don't have any abilities, I'm like everyone else." Peter simply smiled. "You're still having the headaches aren't you?" Robbie nodded, trying to forget. "You're having them for a reason son. You aren't sick, far from it. Look at me." Robbie looked into his father's eyes and knew that he was serious. "Concentrate, concentrate," he said slowly. "I want you to close your eyes and focus on something in the room, anything you want." Robbie closed his eyes and waited. "Good. Now, keep that object in your mind and make it move." "What?" "Trust me." "Dad this is stupid." "Trust me!" Robbie kept his eyes firmly closed and thought about the books behind his father. He concentrated hard and thought about what would happen if they came down from the shelves they were on. He felt silly, like it was some kind of joke. But slowly he became calm, almost sleepy. For a moment he didn't care about the people who made fun of him, or how he felt different to everyone else, he was... happy.

"Ok, open them." Robbie opened his eyes, one after another, as though it had some kind of bearing on whether he'd been successful or not. His heart fluttered. A shiver ran the length of his spine. He sat in awe, in awe of the empty shelves above his father. "Dad?" "Behind you son." Robbie turned in his seat. Above him there were hundreds of books swirling about in the air like slowly turning tornadoes. They swooped and ducked and weaved, their pages flapped like birds' wings so that Robbie could see the words and illustrations inside. He rose to his feet, stood away from his father's desk and reached out to one. It shot into his grasp. He flipped it over and read the cover. *Great Expectations.* Peter sat back and gave a broad smile. "Believe me now?"

Chapter Two

Havisham Hall

(Two Years Later)

Robbie and Lucy Havisham had never met their granddad. Robbie always wanted to, but something or other had always cropped up. There was always some excuse. He did know one thing though; Oswald was on his dad's side, which meant that he had the same abilities that he and Lucy were born with. Robbie often wondered what his granddad's ability was, after all, every Havisham had one, but neither Peter nor Emily would ever tell him. He knew there was only one reason his parents were so secretive. There was something important about Oswald, something more important even than the genius gene.

It wasn't until his granddad's death that Robbie understood how important he really was. "Heart attack" the doctors said. He didn't even receive the news first hand; it came in the form of a television report. "Tycoon tragedy. Reclusive Billionaire Oswald Havisham dies of heart attack aged 78." Robbie had never seen his dad cry before. He thought growing older made stuff like that easier, but it didn't. It didn't take his dad's pain away or the sense of guilt that Robbie felt when he stood looking at him crying in the kitchen and didn't know what to say or how to act. That evening the funeral arrangements were made and condolences were offered. People in black suits emerged from the woodwork to pay their sympathies. They all had the same stupid things to say "terrible loss," "I knew him well," "I'm sorry." Everyone gobbled down triangular sandwiches and moped about the apartment as if they were the ones who had just lost their granddad. Robbie knew half of them just wanted a piece of Havisham Industries, but that had been settled long ago, long before the "Tycoon Tragedy." A few days later it was official, the will came through, and with it, detailed in full, were Oswald's instructions, to leave a mansion, named Havisham Hall to his son Peter, and his immediate family, Emily, Robert, and Lucy Havisham. When the funeral was over and things had settled a little, the Havishams moved from their apartment in the city, to the mansion on Applegate Street. Peter didn't relish the thought, too many painful reminders, but soon their 1942 Cadillac convertible rolled up at the gates of Havisham Hall and the move was underway.

"It's so strange moving back," said Peter dragging the last of the luggage from the Cadillac's boot. Emily stood staring at their new home from the gravel path outside. "I can't imagine you growing up here" she said, wiping dirt from a railing that led to the front door. "It just seems so...well, eerie." Robbie and Lucy bolted ahead and pushed open the giant oak door. Stepping inside they knew they had never seen anything like it. They had moved plenty of times but this place was different, special. "The hallway is the size of our entire old house" beamed Lucy. "Check this out" she said flicking an old suit of armour just to hear the pinging sound. "This is so cool!" shouted Robbie from across the room. He was standing under a dusty old blunderbuss mounted on the wall. Above it there was a stag's head with bulging black eyes that seemed to leer down at them. "Looks like that old bag we saw staring at us from the car" said Lucy arriving beside him, "should have fried her." "Manners Lucy," said Emily coming through the door with two heavy looking cases, "we need to make a good impression on these people." "Mum this is the coolest house ever. I can't believe we're gonna live here." "Neither can I" replied Emily, leaving the cases on the marble floor. "What's the matter Mum?" asked Lucy "Don't you like it?" "Of course I do darling it'll just take some getting used to." Robbie knew his mum was lying, she was uncomfortable. She had never wanted to move, but it was expected of them, it was

Oswald's will. Robbie imagined how his granddad had spent time in Havisham Hall, which rooms he'd been in most, if he had read all of the books stacked on the shelves above them. He looked about and wondered why his granddad had led such a secretive life. It was more than a mystery that drove Robbie's thoughts, it was a need, an urge to discover more about the man that had created Havisham Industries and built the mansion that he was standing in. Although he had never met Oswald, Robbie knew there was a sense of him in the house; his stamp was everywhere. Robbie went to a nearby doorway and peeked through the little gap between the door and the frame into what he assumed was a dining room. There was a long table, dressed in a crisp white cloth, with blue and white cups and saucers on it, and silver cutlery that glistened in the morning sunlight. "Come on," called Emily, "let's look at the rest of this place." Emily and Lucy went up a large staircase that led from the hallway and branched into two at the top. Robbie had one last look around and followed. "What was wrong with granddad," he asked from the foot of the stairs, "why didn't he go outside?" "Oh Rob don't start this again, please." "It's no wonder," said Lucy, "if I lived in this place I wouldn't go outside either." "You do live here idiot." "Shut up Robbie!" Peter dropped his suitcase under the coat rack inside the front door. There was no mystery for him in Havisham Hall, only sadness. For him the mansion was Oswald's, not his, it could never really be his. Emily glanced from the stairs. "I'll be up in a few minutes" she called to Robbie and Lucy. They didn't pay much attention. Robbie took the left branch of the stairs and Lucy took the right.

After around half an hour of exploring, they met up again on the same corridor. "What are you doing?" shouted Lucy from the end of the hall. "Looking for a room!" "Duh, what kind?" "Granddad's, Mum said it was up here." "Here I'll help" said Lucy practically shoving him out of the way. "I don't need your help, Lucy, Lucy quit it." The door came open. "Mine" she announced walking inside. The room was dark, with a marble fireplace in the centre. A diamond encrusted chandelier hung above a huge white shaggy carpet, the kind that usually had a bear's head attached. "Dad said this place was big," she explained "but this is ridiculous." "Granddad was worth billions," offered Robbie "he probably had tons of places like this." Over in the corner, under a little round Victorian window there was an old writing desk with a book on it. Robbie and Lucy crossed their grandfather's room like ghosts in the darkness. "The property of Oswald P. Havisham" said Robbie picking up the book. "Well, open it!" He hesitated. "Maybe we shouldn't look through granddad's stuff." "Chicken, I thought you wanted to know why he was such a weirdo?" "I never said that!" "Robbie stop being such a girl, give it here." Lucy snatched the book from his grasp. It flew out of her grip and landed onto the headless shaggy carpet. "Oh well done." She crouched to retrieve it. Suddenly the book opened and its pages flicked forward. A shaft of smoky green light shot up from the book. She took a panicked step back as a face shimmered and emerged in the hazy green glow, the face of Oswald Havisham. Robbie stepped forward. "Is that, granddad?" "Shush, I think it's some kinda hologram." "This is the visual diary of Oswald P. Havisham" the hologram said. "It is him." "Shush!" "Peter, if you are viewing this, it means that I am gone, and you now control Havisham Industries. But I leave this message for a different purpose. I can only pray that you haven't already found what I have tried to conceal. In the attic there is a device which must never be tampered with, which must never be activated." "So shouldn't be looking at this." "You must promise never to use it Peter, this is absolutely essential. I have kept it from Lombardi and the others, they must never know of its existence. It almost destroyed everything.

I have tried and failed to fulfill my dream son, but do not let my dream become your nightmare." Oswald gave a gentle smile from within the green haze then vanished and the room was cast in darkness. "O.K, what the hell was that?" "We've got to show dad," said Robbie cradling the book in his arms. "No way, he'd freak if he knew we were up here." "You're the one who wanted to open it." "Well I didn't know there was gonna be some old guy in there did I?" "He's not just some old guy, and that message wasn't meant for us." "So, what, you just wanna forget we saw it, you're not even slightly curious?" Robbie laid the book down on the desk and said nothing. "No wonder people think you're weird Robbie, you've got a chance to check out something really cool and you don't even care." Lucy turned her back on her brother. "What was he up to?" she asked hypothetically. "Whatever it was I bet it was..." "Weird?" finished Robbie sarcastically.

Dark grey clouds rolled in over Havisham Hall. Little spits of rain landed on the window as if on cue. Robbie and Lucy rested their elbows on the wooden sill in the gloom and peered down to where the Cadillac lay parked outside. They were up so high that it looked like a toy. "Hey, there she is again" said Lucy squinting to see an old woman outside the gates. The same one she had seen staring at the car on the way to the mansion. "What's she looking at?" The woman looked up as if staring right through them, then she shook her head and moved away. Robbie had the feeling that there was something dark about the mansion, about Oswald's message, but he kept it to himself. "It's too dark in here" he said. "No problemo." A warm wind rolled into the room and rushed around Lucy, blowing her hair into a chaotic dark stream. Beneath her flapping fringe Robbie could see her brown eyes roll back in her head and reappear a pale blue colour. She held out her hand. A ball of flame appeared in it, casting out the darkness. They looked out through the window and down to Applegate Street, their faces lit in the orange glow. Robbie looked at the flame in his sister's palm. "We're not gonna fit in here, are we?"

Chapter Three

THE DREAM STREAMER

idnight. Robbie and Lucy stood outside Havisham Hall. Flames raged around the whole street. "They have no right to take the house!" shouted Lucy. The neighbours approached brandishing sticks and broken bottles. A wall of flame shot between them and the crowd. "Do it!" she roared to her brother. Robbie lowered his head, closed his eyes and sent a shockwave into the gathering. The wave blasted down Applegate Street and launched a row of people into the air. They landed in trees, collided with cars, and slapped hard against the footpath as more closed in. One reached out, catching Robbie's shirtsleeve. "Get outta here you freaks," he said looming down. Lucy fired a flame ball, setting him alight. More rushed in, crowding them. "I can't hold them!" The crowd heaved forward. Their hands reached out. Robbie felt himself being crushed. Suddenly he recognised someone, his old school teacher, Mr Finch. "Wait, what are you doing here?" "I don't know," said Finch "it's your nightmare."

Everything went black. Robbie's bedroom light came sharply into focus. "Rob, Rob wake up. Robbie. You're having a nightmare you idiot, I could hear you from next door." Robbie propped himself against the headboard of his wrought iron bed and breathed a deep sigh of relief. His sheets were soaked through with sweat. "What are you doing in my room?" he said wiping his eyes like nothing had happened. "Couldn't sleep, kept thinking about the hologram." Lucy paused making sure she wanted to say what she was about to say.

"I'm going up there."

"Where?"

"The attic, I wanna see what he was on about."

"Don't be stupid, he said it was dangerous."

"Yeah well, so are we remember."

She headed for the door. "Lucy come back!" It was too late; she'd left the room and disappeared into the darkness of the hallway. Robbie went to the side of his bed and wondered if he should follow. A quick flashback of his nightmare made the decision easier. He took Oswald's book, which he kept by his bedside, pressed his feet to the cold floor, placed them into his slippers and shot out after her.

"Knew you'd change your mind."

A little flame rose in Lucy's palm and they set off down the corridor. Oil paintings of long gone Havishams hung high on the gloomy walls. Their faces loomed down in the fiery glow with disdain. "I still don't think this is a good idea." "You never think anything's a good idea."

DONG... DONG.

"What's that?"

"Relax, it was a clock, stop being such a wuss Robbie."

"You're right, creepy mansion, middle of the night, dangerous experiment we were warned not to go near, what's there to be scared of?"

"Stop being so dramatic, we're not in Scooby Doo."

The staircase to the next level was at the top of the corridor. Everything was deathly quiet. The suits of armour that looked harmless during the day took on a more ominous appearance now, like they were about to walk along by themselves or let out deafening howls through their mouth grills. Robbie could see his breath disappear into the pale moonlight that flooded the hallway. He looked out through one of the old French windows and saw a thick fog descend across Applegate Street. "Come on, we've got to keep moving." Robbie looked up at the sets of stairs that towered above them and disappeared into darkness at the top of the mansion.

"It's gonna take ages to walk up there."

"Got a better idea?"

"Yeah actually"

"No Robbie, not again." Robbie closed his eyes. "Robbie!" Slowly they lifted off of the ground and floated into the air. Lucy jammed her eyes shut as they drifted up through the gap in the sets of stairs, up through the levels, up and up into the air until the floor they had taken off from was almost impossible to see. Robbie opened his eyes as they came close to the ceiling. "We're almost there, hang on." He raised his hand up in front of Lucy who still had her eyes shut tight and gently pushed her back through the air, she glided across under the roof and came to rest on the landing. She found herself beneath the door that led into the attic. "Great, it's barred." "Step back." Robbie snapped the lock. Lucy shot impatiently up the stairs and pushed open the door. "Shush, you're gonna wake Mum and Dad." The attic was pitch black but for a round window that let a circular patch of moonlight onto the dusty wooden floorboards. She crept as carefully and quietly as she could across the lab, gazing in awe at the cobwebbed devices around her, each bizarre one reflected in her upraised eyes. "These things are seriously creepy." "You're the one who wanted to come up here," said Robbie from behind. "I know, I didn't think it'd be this weird though. I can't believe he made billions from all this gross stuff." Robbie wanted to tell her that it wasn't gross, but it was no use trying to tell Lucy anything. There were metallic skeletons with long twisty arms draped in cobwebs and there were circuit boards and wires that hung down from tall boxes. Robbie gazed at the collection of old experiments and wondered how many years had gone into them, how many times had Oswald felt like giving up, was he the kind that gave up? Robbie noticed Oswald's diary glowing under his arm. He looked at the cover, it read, OPEN ME.

"Hey, look at this."

Lucy eyed the book warily, half expecting another hologram to leap from its pages. Robbie unfastened its golden clasps and opened it from the back. Written on old yellowy paper was a long list of invention names, neurolisers, physio phasers, skeleton transmitters, they went on and on. "What kinda messed up names are they?" asked Lucy peering over his shoulder. At the bottom of the page sat two lonely words. Dream Streamer. "Dream Streamer" said Robbie aloud. "You what?" "A Dream Streamer, I think it's what Granddad was working on, what he meant in that message." "What's a Dream Streamer?" asked Lucy.

"No idea, something to do with dreams I guess."

"How astute"

"You asked."

"Well, great, how are we supposed to find it in all this junk?" "I don't think we'll have to" said Robbie. The book tugged against Robbie's grasp like a feral cat, shot free, and landed on the ground. Lucy stared in amazement as it set off by itself along the lab floor. "It's trying to tell us something." "Seriously, what's the deal with books in this place?" Lucy fell in behind her brother. "What's it doing?" "Leading the way. When I said Dream Streamer it just took off." "Living books, great." The book led them past mounds of hydraulic parts, around stacks of pistons, springs and gauges and across the lab. As though they were being guided further and further into a bizarre jungle of steel, wood and wire. The book slowed, then stopped at a huge pile of metal parts. "Well, where is it?" "It should be right here." "Wait a sec," said Lucy stepping out "I think I see it." She reached out using the flame as a guide. Up ahead, in a hollow carved out of the wall, there sat a machine, a machine in the shape of a beehive. It was different from the rusty browns and oranges of the scrap metal around it; it had a translucent green tint. "What is that thing?" Robbie could see it too. It had hammered metal panels all around it and nuts and bolts stuck out from the sides. Lucy crept up and hunkered down beside it. She could barely see an inscription on its side but it was covered by dirt that had built up around it. She drew her sleeve over her hand and used it to wipe away the grime. Suddenly the inscription became clear.

BOG OFF NOSEY

"Guess he had a sense of humour then."

Robbie walked forward and picked up the living book from the floor. "Why would he build this thing and then just lock it up here?" asked Lucy, "it doesn't make any sense." "You heard what he said," answered Robbie "it's dangerous." "My God Robbie, change the CD, not everything's dangerous you know. Don't you ever wonder why we never came here, why we never saw him?" "I know why. He was sick." "That was just stuff Mum and Dad said to stop us from coming here. Don't be so naive" Lucy stood up, wiped the dust from her hands onto her black dress and went to pry open the Dream Streamer's huge chamber door. "What are you doing?" "You can be chicken if you want but I wanna find the truth."

"Lucy don't!"

Lucy went inside the Dream Streamer. There was a black leather chair. She looked around at the green metal walls and slouched comfortably into the seat. It was like being inside her own private spaceship. Except there were no buttons or levers, in fact, there was nothing at all, nothing but a seat and an odd looking metal box situated overhead. "Maybe Granddad wasn't such a weirdo after all... see, nothing to worry about."

SLAM

The hatch closed. Lucy darted up and tried the door. Panic shot across her face. "Robbie!" she shouted silently from within the hive. A green glow started up in the chamber. Robbie stepped closer, pressing his hands to the glass panel over the door. He banged on the cold metal and tried to pry open the hatch. It was no use. It wouldn't budge. Through the glass he could see translucent green energy streams rise from Lucy's head. Robbie could make out images in the streams as they drifted up and disappeared through the metal box above her. He could see frightening images of everything she had ever been afraid of, snakes, weird looking faces, things she had seen on TV, things that she hadn't spoken about. It was as if her dreams were being sucked out of her head, no, not her dreams, her nightmares. Her face twitched under the strange light as they rose and vanished. She looked scared and small, as if the Dream Streamer was about to swallow her up. It started to shake, rattling the floorboards as the nightmares were extracted. Test tubes and Bunsen burners hopped off of their tables and smashed onto the floor. Robbie was sure the sound would wake his parents below.

WHAM

A blast of light shot from the Dream Streamer and across the lab. Blinded, he hit the floor. A crackle of blue electricity swept over the Dream Streamer and tongues of lightning shot out overhead. Everything fell silent.

Silence... just silence. After a moment Robbie lowered his hand from his eyes and looked up at the Dream Streamer, now full of a hazy smoke. It was powering down and the glow inside the chamber faded until there was nothing but darkness. It had all happened in seconds.

Swooooosh.

The chamber opened letting out a thick grey cloud of vapour that spread across the floor. A black figure rose up in the Dream Streamer and made its way through the haze. Robbie stood in silence ready to confront whatever emerged, the book in one hand, a clenched fist on the other side, too many scary movies.

The figure came closer. Robbie's chest tightened in fear. He half expected Lucy to appear grotesque and disfigured. After a few moments the long shadow in the vapour shrank and Lucy emerged, drained and barely conscious. She staggered to a nearby experiment and almost fainted. "What happened in there?" asked Robbie. Lucy stayed silent, then turned slowly and said just three words. "I feel, lighter."

Chapter Four

ENTER THE CIRCLE

THE NEXT MORNING

Applegate Street felt like everybody in the neighbourhood had been possessed by aliens. Everything seemed too "perfect", too similar. Even the way people spoke and moved was the same. They had the same cars in their driveways, the same number of children, the same pretty manicured lawns and the same pink garden sheds. This would never change.

Emily despised the place, but she knew that she'd have to meet the neighbours at some stage. She stood outside No. 28, the house belonged to Matthew and Gretchen Oldham. Mrs Oldham arrived at the door with pink curlers buried in her greasy hair and a cigarette clutched tightly between her withered lips. "Yes?" she said, like her throat was full of stones. "Hello, my name is Emily, Emily Havisham." "I know who you are," snapped Oldham "you're related to Oswald. He was that scientist," she said gesturing up the hill to the mansion. "Did you know him well?" asked Emily. "Too well, we all knew him, or knew of him. Up in that little room." Emily knew she was referring to the lab. "Bit of a shut in, never spoke to anyone. Seemed to think he was better than other people, supposedly very intelligent. If you ask me he was daft as a brush, but that happens to those intelligent types doesn't it? They don't know how to relate to people" she said dragging on her cigarette and blowing its smoke into Emily's face. "What does your husband do?" Emily would have preferred to gouge her own eyes out rather than tell her. "Peter is a scientist," she said almost apologetically. "Ha, another scientist. They seem to follow you around Ms Havisham." "Mrs Havisham" corrected Emily. "My Matthew is a bank manager, we don't have a mansion or the money you must have but we get by well enough. You know how it is, or perhaps you don't." "Yes, of course." "He grew up in there didn't he, your husband." "Oh, yes, he did." "Always such a quiet boy, so secretive. Come to think of it they were all quiet. It must have been difficult when his mother died." "I'm sure it was, but that was a long time ago." "She was a beautiful woman, I could never understand what she saw in Oswald. Then again money is a powerful incentive isn't it?" Emily didn't reply. "You look well, you don't have their paleness. The Havishams I mean. They all had it didn't they?" Another question that was too stupid to answer. "Yes, beautiful, I love your hair," she commented with a cringe worthy falseness "Oh and those vintage dresses that you wear, simply delightful." "Thank you" replied Emily, searching for a way out of the uncomfortable situation. "Well, I better be getting back... it was nice to meet you, hopefully I'll see you again sometime." "Indeed" replied Oldham, her eyes fixed on Emily's as she slowly closed out her pink front door. "That went well" whispered Emily to herself as she went to cross the road. The streets were quiet and full of golden autumn leaves; only the sound of crows cawing above could be heard.

"You have no place here Mrs Havisham," came a voice from behind, a voice that didn't belong to Mrs Oldham. "Your new home, it is trouble." "Who are you?" said Emily turning around. She stood before an old woman who wore a dark dress with a floral pattern. There was a faded red ribbon in her hair. The old woman looked familiar, but Emily couldn't tell from where or when she had seen her before. "I am only someone who is concerned for your well being," said the old woman "and the well being of your family." "You know nothing about my family," replied Emily angrily. "Don't I? Emily Havisham?" Emily's heart skipped a beat, her face drained white. "On the contrary I know everything about you. I know about

Peter, and the children, about their abilities. Do you know that they are in serious danger?" "Stay away, I'm warning you." "I don't have long to explain this Emily, so please listen carefully. It is imperative that Oswald's machine be dismantled." "Who are you? " "You truly have no idea, do you?" "Look, I don't know where you've come from, but if you don't leave my family and I alone I'll call the police." "Mrs Havisham after what I've been through, do you really think police frighten me? Oh, if I could only tell you the truth of our situation, if I could only open your eyes to the danger in that house." I'm not listening to this!" "I have risked my life to speak to you Mrs Havisham, please grant me the indulgence of fulfilling my task." "What!" "Destroy the machine, please. Think of your children." The old woman then turned and vanished, as if into thin air.

Lucy watched everything from her bedroom window; it was the same old woman that she'd seen before.

But that didn't bother her. Not as much as the pain rising in the pit of her stomach. She slouched back in the brown leather armchair beneath her window and tried to concentrate on her book. A cold clammy sweat came over her as she focused on the print. Her head felt like it was in a slowly tightening vice and her stomach churned round and round. She put down the book and walked out of her room onto the corridor. A walk will do me good she thought. After a few paces the ill feelings increased, like hunger pains. She gazed up at the walls that were cluttered with oil on canvas portraits. They were paintings of relatives that had lived with the genius gene long before her. Relatives that had probably felt the way she felt sometimes, that resented the genius gene as she did. As if being a twelve-year-old girl wasn't tough enough without being a human inferno into the bargain. Lucy went further down the hall. A ray of sunlight came in through a window, illuminating a portrait of Oswald. She gazed up at his kind but oddly ominous appearance. The pain stabbed at her again, as if returning at the thought of him. If she were being honest, ever since she'd moved to Havisham Hall she'd felt as uneasy as her mum. The pain grew worse. Lucy knew what was causing it, or at least had a good idea. It was the machine, the Dream Streamer. It was strange, the more she thought of it, the more she wanted to see it again. She had a curious sensation to go back up there, back to the attic, back to the Dream Streamer, back to the danger.

Havisham Hall was so large that Robbie had gotten lost in it three times after breakfast, but no matter which room he went into, the gigantic library, the cinema room, or the swimming pool in the basement his mind kept wandering back to the message in Oswald's diary. That night he went to sleep with his head full of thoughts of Oswald, the Dream Streamer, and the living book that sat safely on the shelves above his bed.

VREEEEEEER

Robbie awoke to the sound at midnight and saw the wall beside his bed glowing green. The light was coming from somewhere in the room. He didn't want to look at first; he thought it might be a ghost, or something worse. Slowly he peeked over his blankets. The living book was glowing under a pile of clothes on the floor. He hopped out of bed, cleared away his socks and shirts from the pile and picked it up. On the brown leather cover there was a green question mark, fading in and out like fairy lights. He snatched it up quickly and scattered back to bed, heart thumping in his chest. He unfastened the golden clasps once more and the light stopped. For a moment there was only darkness. Then the book glowed under his covers casting Robbie-shaped shadows up on the walls around his bed. The pages flicked to the centre again like before, and started to shimmer like ripples in a pond. Oswald's face appeared. "So, we meet at last.

Face to face, or at least face to book." "Granddad?"
"Robert Havisham, my grandson. I thought this day
might never come... but here we are, well, there you
are... I am, well, I'm not here am I? "Is it really you?"
"Well of course it's really me, you didn't think I'd go
and die without leaving something behind did you?"
Oswald had a kindly face, full of wrinkles and creases,
evidence of a life's work. He didn't look like Robbie's
dad. He was more laid back, more fun looking. "I am
sure there is a lot you want to know Robert, this book
is a guide to the things which I have left behind, things
which I could never tell you personally." "What's a
Dream Streamer?" blurted Robbie, like it was the
only thing on his mind. Oswald's expression turned
to a cold concern. "Robert, that machine is not to be
touched, it is not to be interfered with. You should
never have even seen it." "But what is it? I mean what
does it do?" "I designed the Dream Streamer many
years ago, when I was younger, and a lot more alive

than I am today. The Dream Streamer was designed to destroy nightmares, to take every frightening thought from a person's mind and make it disappear. I created it so that no one need ever be afraid to dream." "But, that's a good thing." "It would have been, if something hadn't gone wrong." "What, what happened?" Oswald didn't answer. "Granddad?" "There are some things that people shouldn't know Robert. As you know you are not holding an ordinary book, but then again you are not an ordinary boy are you? There are many secrets between these pages, which have never been seen by human eyes. Which can never be seen by anyone but you. I am sure your father has told you about the genius gene, about Jeremiah and our family history, but he hasn't told you everything. There is so much more to learn before you go exploring hubs and Holocites. Leave the Dream Streamer alone Robert, it is dangerous, more dangerous than you realise." Robbie wanted to ask Oswald what Holocites were and tell him about Lucy, but he didn't have the heart and asked a different question instead, a question that he'd wanted answered for a long time. "Why couldn't we visit you?" Oswald smiled faintly. "I've often wondered the same thing Robert, let's just say that I kept odd company while I was alive." "What's that supposed to mean?" "Your father never told you about the Circle, did he?" "What Circle?" "I thought so. The complexities of the Circle are far too numerous and important to mention here, instead I have left directions for you, to follow, to keep secret, and to never mention to another human soul. It is a secret which your father has kept for years and which I trust you to keep now." "The Circle is a place?" Oswald smiled. "It is a place, a thing, the future and the past all rolled into one." "Could you be any more mysterious?" "This book will tell you much, but the rest is out there, in a world which I know you are afraid of, I know because I was afraid too. I know what it's like to be different Robert." Robbie knew he was looking at a hologram, but it felt like his granddad was talking to him in person, like he really knew him. "The genius gene is part of your DNA, it is who you are. You should never be ashamed of that." But Robbie knew that it wasn't that simple, his life wasn't that of a superhero. It was the life of a boy with a terrible secret, a secret that threatened to destroy him if it was ever revealed. "I must go now," said Oswald, "but rest assured, when you need help I will be here between the pages of this book." "Wait." "Trust me Robert, the book is the key." The image of Oswald distorted and shimmered again, like ripples in reverse. The pages flicked backwards and the book closed in Robbie's hands. Oswald was gone. On the cover a new symbol shone, an arrow, directing him out of bed. For a second Robbie thought of what his mum and dad would do if they found him out of his room. He had to take the chance, if he didn't he'd never know the truth. He hopped out, pulled on his clothes and followed the living book to the window. The book launched out of his hands and nudged open the crosshatched glass panels. Robbie looked down at the houses on Applegate Street, then at the book. On the cover there were two words.

HOLD ON

Wham. In a flash he was whipped out through his bedroom window and took off across the night sky. Gripping the book for dear life he looked down at Applegate Street and the hill leading into town as it got smaller and smaller and he was taken higher and higher into the cloudy sky. The air was freezing, the wind blasted against his face, but he didn't care, he'd floated before, but nothing like this, nothing this fast. Car lamps looked like stars on the streets beneath, like he was sandwiched between the stars above and the stars below. He looked ahead and saw the books arrow pointing the way, to where he had no idea. He didn't care; he was free of snooty old women, bossy sisters and nightmares. Robbie flew over London and wondered if anyone could spot him from the streets below, a ten-year-old boy clutching a book while zooming through the sky. If people thought he was weird before this would have finished him. The London Eye looked odd from his position in the sky, like it was just a dot in the immensity of the bustling metropolis. He shot further along and in no time he was passing over the houses of parliament. The sounds of the city rose up. Buses, car horns, conversations, snippets of music filled the air and were quickly gone. Where he was going there were less lights and hardly any life. The book began to lower in his hands and he felt himself gliding toward the road. The streets were empty and quiet in this place. It looked like an industrial estate. For some reason he didn't think the book would lead him somewhere like this, a place so dead and empty. Robbie hit the road unsteadily and tumbled slightly before correcting himself. He looked down at the book, there was a name written on the cover, Samuel Barber. The light faded out.

Robbie found himself outside a dirty little shop. Paint flaked away from a large golden sign outside which read Sam Barber's Science Supplies. Its front window wore a thick layer of dust and there was a collection of dead blue bottles visible from outside. He paused for a moment, shaken, and wondered what was waiting for him inside.

Chapter Five

SAMUEL BARBER

*L*ucy's vision blurred as she staggered up the wooden steps at the top of Havisham Hall, they seemed never ending. The attic was far out of reach; with Robbie gone she couldn't just hover up there and walk inside like she'd done before. Lucy's thoughts became a confused mess, as though she wasn't in control, as if something else wanted her to return to the Dream Streamer. She was being led somewhere, dragged forward like a puppet on invisible strings. Her pupils turned pale blue. There was no way to break loose, no way of going back. Somehow the closer she got to the Dream Streamer the better she felt, as though she'd only ever feel OK again if she was near the machine. She came to the base of the next floor, looked up with those pale blue eyes and climbed the steps, the steps to the Dream Streamer.

Robbie entered Samuel's *Science Supplies* and was overcome with a strong damp smell, like heaps of old washing had been laid out. Above him, in the gloom, stacks of science equipment lay on woodworm ridden shelves. Robbie could see spiders climb thin webs that reflected in the moonlight like strands of an old woman's hair. Suddenly a clanking sound came from the back of the shop. Robbie could see someone move about. "Samuel? Samuel Barber?" Silence. There was a faint rustle. Robbie looked up and thought the heaving shelves were about to fall down on top of him. There was another rustle and the sound of clanking metal. Then slowly, out of the blackness, he appeared. Samuel Barber peeked over the large wooden counter at the back of his shop. A head of frizzy orange hair sat atop his out of breath face. He had a large bushy moustache and wore old tattered clothes that were covered in a white powdery dust, like he was part of the furniture, and just as creaky. Samuel stuck his hand into his grubby shirt pocket to fetch his double-glazed glasses and let out a cough that sent the dust on his clothes puffing up into the air. He stopped, wiped some breadcrumbs from his moustache and squinted over the counter. "Who aw you?" he asked, analysing Robbie like he had discovered a new species of bug. "I'm Robbie... Robbie Havisham." "Haw," came a loud over the top laugh "another one eh, just what we need, haw haw." Robbie hated when people laughed at their own jokes, especially when they weren't funny. "Wait a minute," said Samuel in sudden realisation "you're Oswald's grandson awn't you?" Robbie nodded. "Well, that's different then. Quite different indeed. Came along for a visit did you old chap, or young chap in this case." "Well, um." Samuel moved from behind his desk and the clanging sound started up again. It was the same noise Robbie's dad made when rummaging around in his toolbox. Samuel emerged from behind the grubby old counter. Robbie's heart froze. He stood in shock at the sight before him. Samuel's top half looked almost normal with his crusty old cardigan and big ginger moustache, but where his legs should have been there were a pair of black robotic stabilisers that stomped the floor like a wild horse. Like a centaur, a myth, a legend. But this was no myth, no legend.

SCREEG SCREEG

Pistons, springs and hydraulics moved in Samuel's mechanical legs as he walked, or stomped along. Robbie half expected him to snort steam. "Before you ask, yes they are real. I presume you've never seen a Centaborg before?" "But, they can't be..." "What, real? Young Havisham where we're going the word real doesn't apply. Your grandfather mustn't have told you a lot about this place." "Never met him," snapped Robbie as though he'd been insulted. "Ah, that would explain a thing or two, as I recall he was quite meticulous about privacy, yes, yes, especially when it came to family." Robbie thought of his dad and how he was the same way. "Your granddad and I were the best of friends," said Samuel, "he was a brilliant man, a good man. If I ever had a problem he was the one I went to. He was the one who taught me about the Circle you know." "What is the Circle exactly?" "Ah, all in good time young Havisham. First you must tell me about you. How have you come to be here for example, hum?" Robbie wasn't sure if he could trust Samuel, but he went ahead and told him anyway. "Well, you see there was a book, a kind of diary that belonged to my granddad, it told me to come here." "Was it brown, with your grandfather's initials etched into it by any chance?" "Yeah, why?" "They are what are known as soul echoes. "I called my granddad's a living book." "Haw haw, well, quite a good name actually, and perhaps more accurate than you realise. In a way they are alive, in another they are not. Soul echoes store little bits of consciousness inside their pages, they have memories and can respond to certain things, but ask them questions that stray too far from the path and they have no idea what you're talking about. People leave them behind for their loved ones as a way to keep their memory alive, literally. It's all a bit complicated, the important thing is that you are here, and if Oswald asked you to come it must be for something special. You know, you look a lot like him Robbie. You have his eyes in fact." Robbie looked embarrassed yet proud at the same time. "I have my grandfather's eyes too" said Samuel reaching under the counter. He produced a jar with a set of pickled eyeballs. Robbie froze in shock. "I think his hand may be around here too." Robbie inched away from Samuel. "Oh don't look so shocked young Havisham, it's quite normal for Centaborgs to leave little pieces of themselves after death." "Mr Barber," asked Robbie hesitantly "are there more like you, Centaborgs I mean." "There were, there were millions of us, billions maybe, but our numbers have dwindled over the years, things happened, dark things, things that..." Samuel looked away for a moment, as if it was too painful to finish the sentence. "Anyways, enough of that" he said breaking the silence. Samuel clanked his way to a large dusty bookcase that stood at the end of the gloomy room. "Wait, where are you going?" "You wanted to see the Circle didn't you, well, this is the way."

Samuel reached through an opening in the rows of books, grabbed a handle and gave it a quick jolt. The enormous bookcase shifted from its position and moved across the floor. After a moment it came to a halt, a large gaping hole lay hollowed out in the wall. Samuel went through first. Robbie stood at the mouth of the entrance, peering into the dark. "Young man the entrance doesn't stay open forever you know." Robbie had a bad feeling in the pit of his stomach; then again he felt that way most of the time. He blew his fringe out of his eyes and went into the darkness. He watched as the bookcase moved back into position, sealing them in. Two powerful lights came on at the sides of

Samuel's legs. "Handy little things, our technicians installed them a few months ago. Well then, ready for the most amazing adventure of your life young Havisham?" Robbie looked down at the stone steps that led deep down into the bowels of the building. He thought of Oswald. "Yeah, I'm ready."

Chapter Six

GOIN UNDERGROUND

It was late at night when Emily got the chance to speak to Peter. He had been working late in the downtown labs. After all it fell to him to run Havisham Industries now. "You're late again" she called from the kitchen table. "Sorry darling" came Peter's voice echoing around the walls and marble floor of the hallway. "One of the generators went down, took hours to repair." "I took a walk around the neighbourhood" called Emily. Peter entered the room. "You met Oldham then?" "Mrs Oldham isn't the one I'm worried about." "What do you mean?" "An old woman told me today that we're in danger, that this place is dangerous, is that true?" Darling, what are you talking about?" "Don't darling me. She knew all of us Peter, she knew my name. How could she have known that?" Peter looked as confused as Emily.

"What did she say?" "She knew about the children's abilities, and yours, she said that they were in danger, she said something about a Dream Streamer." Peter looked stunned. Emily spotted his reaction immediately, though he tried to conceal it. "What does that mean Peter, what's a Dream Streamer?" "It's nothing, it's just an idea that my dad had, it's not possible. He tried for years to create a Dream Streamer, it didn't work, it couldn't, not with him lurking around." "Who, who's him, please don't tell me you're mixed up with those Circle people again. We promised not to keep secrets from each other." "The Circle have saved us more times than I can count. They're not the problem." "Peter Havisham, if you don't tell me everything you know this instant!" "Look, I don't know anything about an old woman, that's the truth." "And the Dream Streamer? She seemed to think it was here, in the mansion." "No, that's impossible. You knew my father, he'd never leave something like that here." "Well I'm not comfortable, God knows who she is or what she's capable of, what if she's told someone about the children?" Peter went to his wife and wrapped his arms around her. "Don't worry. Everything's going to be fine. By the way, where are the children?"

A sliver of moonlight came through the attic's oval window, illuminating the Dream Streamer. It looked ominous and strange. The attic was silent but for Lucy's footsteps crossing the wooden floor boards. Her eyes beamed bright rays of light onto the green metal shell. Part of her remembered Oswald's message, the human side maybe, but she couldn't resist. She went to the back of the Dream Streamer where she knew the activation switch was, but she didn't know, she couldn't have known, they weren't her memories, they were somebody else's. She wrestled to take her hand away from the switch but it shot forward and turned it.

VRRROOOOM

The Dream Streamer began to purr. It lay charging in the attic, Lucy's nightmares guarded inside. A hive, sitting, humming, in the dark. A ticking time bomb.

Robbie and Samuel followed the steps further and further underground. Robbie noticed names etched into the ancient walls. "Previous members," Samuel said, sensing the question coming. "How many are there now?" "In this branch you mean? Around a thousand I'd imagine, but the number changes all the time. It's not like the old days, I remember when only ten or twenty were good enough to meet the standards, now they come from everywhere. Dumbing down of the organisation if you awsk me. No offence intended of course, if you're anything like Oswald you must have brains to burn." "Lucy's job" said Robbie ducking under a bit of jagged rock. As they cleared the steps Robbie found himself in an open cavern that went on forever. There were rocks, puddles, cracks and crevices all across the stony ground. "This place rocks" said Robbie jokingly.

"Indeed," said Samuel with an upraised eyebrow "I suppose it does. These caves are where the first Circle meetings were held, almost 500 years ago. They have seen geniuses like Alfons Serafinowicz, William S Maracovey, David Riddle, Oswald Havisham." "This is it?" asked Robbie incredulously "this is the Circle?" "The actual Circle? God no, the headquarters are, well, let's just say a bit more high tech than this, and a damn sight brighter. Come along, we've got a way to go." The walls were wet, slippery, they changed colour as Robbie and Samuel passed by, shining like serpent skin, like the whole place was alive. Samuel went out ahead. It was clear that he had his own path, it was clear that he had done this many times before. "Careful here, bit of a pothole." Samuel walked under a stone archway and left the alien landscape behind. Robbie followed. Suddenly there was nothing but darkness. This place was different from the rest of the caves, there was clay underfoot. Robbie knew there was a cliff edge ahead, or at least a long drop because as he walked along the clay flew from his shoes and he could hear it rustle at the end of a pit. Not exactly the pothole that Samuel had described. He stopped. "This way old chap." To the side there was a narrow path that reached across the abyss. Samuel's mechanical legs caught slivers of light from a lamp somewhere on the far side. The rocky ground was unsteady and narrow but Samuel wasn't fazed by the fact that his legs could give way and he could plummet to his death below. He was weird, but a good kind of weird. "We've come to an important juncture, as of now we are officially under Big Ben, which means that round this corner we should see the door." Robbie could barely contain his excitement. "Your grandfather was quite the scientist Robbie, always cooking up something or the other, he'd be proud to see you here. Last I heard he was experimenting with dreams." "Nightmares" replied Robbie flatly. "That's right, that's quite right, he

60

thought he could cure them or some such thing. Made something called a, a..." "Dream Streamer" finished Robbie. Robbie didn't want to discuss it, he wanted to forget about it, besides, Oswald had wanted it kept secret. "Well whatever he was working on, it certainly peeked Lombardi's interest." Robbie remembered the name from Oswald's message. "Who's Lombar..." "Here we are," interrupted Samuel, and he walked toward a light shining from the end of a long corridor that was carved from the ancient rock. Robbie reminded himself to ask who Lombardi was again. He didn't want to let it go, besides, he hated when people ignored his questions. At the end of the corridor stood a wooden door with a big thick black wrought iron handle. "Go ahead," said Samuel "Oh, and knock six times." Robbie wrapped on it, counting the knocks in his head, and waited. Nothing happened. "Why did I have to knock six times?" "You didn't" said Samuel "I just get a kick out of people doing that." Keys jangled from the other side and slowly the wooden door creaked open. A blast of intense light flooded the corridor. "After you" said Samuel gesturing inside. From the moment Robbie's feet left the cold rocky ground of the cave and landed on the black marble floor beyond the door he knew he was entering another world. It couldn't have been any less like the series of cold dark tunnels they'd negotiated to get there. He walked along the corridor and saw bright oval lights embedded into the walls on either side, as if he'd just boarded an alien ship. The smooth curved walls were creamy in colour and looked almost plastic in texture, and there was soothing music coming in over an intercom system, like whale music. Robbie stood in awe, "This place is..." "I know, isn't it?" There were large white hatches under the lights that opened up occasionally and let people out. Up ahead, Robbie could see people bustling around, like crowds at airport departure gates. When he walked into the open area he saw the full enormity of the place. Robbie looked up at the walls and saw people working in little holes that were hollowed out of the structure like honey combs. They went all the way up into the air and disappeared into where he presumed the roof was, he couldn't tell for sure because it was obscured by a thick white cloud floating above him at the top levels. There were more offices under the glass floor beneath his feet. "These tunnels go on for miles" informed Samuel. "What is this place, I mean, what do you do down here?" "Well, you could say we're a paranormal taskforce."

"Like, Ghostbusters?"

"Haw, eh, not quite no."

"What's the difference?"

"Well, for one thing we're real."

"What's the other thing?"

"Look around you."

Robbie knew exactly what he meant. It was like there was a new civilization built under ground, a subterranean world. "Every member of the Circle has their own space to work in, their own personal computer and lab coat," explained Samuel leading the way "but the perks go a lot deeper than that, with full membership you get to fight demons, werewolves, zombies, the usuals, you know." The clatter of typing echoed around the walls as they shuffled through the crowd. Robbie noticed people eyeing him strangely, some moved out of the way. He walked on regardless and kept his head down as much as curiosity would allow. "Don't mind them young Havisham, they're just taking a peek. It always happens with new arrivals. CAREFUL!"

Robbie looked ahead and saw the air in front of him change, it shifted into different shapes, bended, distorted. "Step back" warned Samuel. A gust of wind rushed against Robbie's face. There was a white flash and a swirling blue entrance appeared. "It's a portal" said Samuel. Suddenly a man stepped through, as if from nowhere. He tipped his hat to them both and walked down the corridor. Before the portal closed a head appeared, though not a human one. A creature with black eyes that receded into his head and had little slits for nostrils stopped, blinked, then tapped a button at its neck and disappeared back inside. "Who the, what the..?" "Portal guardians" said Samuel. "Only exist to open portals, very handy in a spot of bother. Can be summoned with these nifty old things, or well, new things actually." Samuel produced a device from a shiny compartment in his right leg. "Wonderful bit of kit, can summon up to three guardians at any one time." "Magic" said Robbie. "Not magic lad, science." "I can't believe my granddad knew about this place." "Knew about it? He practically created our new and improved little London branch." "London branch," said Robbie "you mean there are more places like this?" "Well of course, the Circle is worldwide." "Samuel you said the Circle are a paranormal taskforce." "Indeed

I did." "But there aren't any such things as demons and zombies. I mean, they're just made up." "Not true young Havisham. The general rule is, the things you think don't exist do, and the things you think do exist sometimes don't." "You sound like my granddad." "Haw haw, not surprising, Oswald made quite the impression down here." "So, what you're trying to tell me is, my granddad fought monsters?" "Well, in a word, yes." "This is too weird." "On the contrary young Havisham, things haven't even started to get weird."

Chapter Seven

HYSTERIA AT HAVISHAM HALL

Lucy looked on as the green glow spread from inside the Dream Streamer and built up around it like a force field. A horrible clicking sound started. A ball of flame rose in her palm. Rapidly it spread up her arm then quickly engulfed her entire body. Lucy stood in flames and the Dream Streamer clicked its last click.

Midnight

A colossal blast ripped through the lab blowing out the window. It shattered the Dream Streamer into a thousand fragments. A shockwave spread from Havisham Hall like a mushroom cloud. Green light shot from the attic like forks of lightning, then turned to gas in the air and went into each of the chimneys on Applegate Street. It swept through each house taking the nightmares of the streets children with it. Lucy's nightmares drifted from the remains of the Dream Streamer and up into the night air. There the gas formed into different shapes. Changed, changed into living breathing nightmares. They gathered in a swirling Circle, their twisting bodies danced against the light of the moon. Grey rags dripped from their bones as they howled into the night and bared their sharp yellow teeth. One by one the terrors trapped in the minds of Applegate's children made their way up to join them. Children peeked out from behind their bedroom curtains at the nightmares gathered on the street outside. Some nightmares were thin and tall with horrific expressions on their faces, like they had been stretched down in agony, their eyeballs were on the verge of falling out of their sockets. Their bony hands dragged along the ground and the flesh wore away from their knuckles as they went. Others were fat angry looking creatures with bulging veins in their necks and hard tight muscles that were ready to do damage. These nightmares had fury in their hate filled eyes. Others held their heads in their crumbling hands and shuffled like zombies along the dead streets. The sky became so packed and dense with flying bat like creatures that not a single star could be seen above. Each of the lights on Applegate Street went out. People cowered in fear and stayed in their houses. The pillar of terrifying creatures that wriggled about in the air widened and swelled and howled. Smoke billowed out from behind Lucy who stood in the lab window. She looked at her collection of nightmares, her monsters, her pets, and smiled. She wasn't Lucy Havisham anymore, she was something else. In the midst of all of the chaos a single human being walked the streets. It was the old woman that Lucy had seen before. She stood on the path outside Havisham Hall, her hands covering her mouth in shock. She stared into the night, the night full of nightmares.

Robbie and Samuel walked under an arch that led to a gigantic chamber. All around there were computer screens and alcoves where people worked sorting papers. Robbie looked at the glass floor beneath him and could see people putting them into great big hessian sacks. A huge sign hung overhead.

INTEL CENTRE: NO UNCLASSIFIED PERSONNEL BEYOND THIS POINT

Samuel handed Robbie a location device. It had a digital map of all of the tunnels and corridors in the HQ. "May come in handy old chap, it's more than a little easy to get lost down here. Do me a favour would you, take this." Samuel reached into his leg and took out another black device that had dials and digits and wires sticking from everywhere. A materialiser. Similar to the one he'd used to summon the portal guardians. "Point it over there and press that little button thingy on the top" Robbie pressed the button and a swirling pool of energy stretched out into a portal before them.

"Wait, where are you going?" "I have work to do young Havisham, besides your grandfather wanted me to show you this place. He didn't mention babysitting." Samuel stepped through the portal and vanished. Robbie watched the last bit of blue close up.

THUD

Something moved behind. Robbie turned, slowly and nervously, heart pounding in his chest. He found himself surrounded. Different beings of all shapes and sizes stood around him in a Circle, staring, as if they were inspecting him. Many faces, many eyes, all focused on him. "I believe this is who we've been waiting for," came a voice from the crowd. "No, too short!" "He's too pale, too human" came another voice. Robbie glanced at the creatures flanking him on either side. One had gills, pale blue skin and a water tank on its head that sloshed about as he walked along on stilt like legs, another whose body was controlled by a tiny slug that sat in its back. Little mouse like creatures scurried along the floor clutching mini sheets of paper. This was the Circle, this is what Oswald meant, this was insane. One creature stepped from the crowd, a goliath standing 8ft tall with grey leathery skin, and a pair of huge and tough looking hooves. "Welcome human" came a deep booming voice, though gentler somehow than Robbie was expecting. "Eh, hi." Creatures crept around either side of the huge grey being. "I am Sarugril, please excuse my colleagues, they are simply curious." Robbie felt like asking why, but he just stood gazing in awe. "They have never seen a boy over grounder before." "Over grounder? Oh, you mean people from up there" said Robbie pointing upward. "We mean no offence by the term." Robbie wasn't about to argue. "I am a Holocite. We were born in these caves many many years ago. May I ask, what is your business here? It seems unlikely that you came alone." "I..., Samuel showed me down" said Robbie not quite believing what he was seeing. "Ah, Barber, yes. Are you a relation of his perhaps?" "No, I'm here because of..." The story was far too long to recount. "I'm here because of my granddad" settled Robbie. "Which elder over grounder do you speak of?" "Oswald." The beast's ears pricked up. "Oswald Havisham?" "Yeah. Why?" Sarugril stared in fascination. "You are Oswald's favourite." "I, I am?" "We are honoured to have you among us Robert." "Wait, how do you know my name?" "We know much about you." "But, I never even knew this place existed until today." "Oswald has spoken fondly of you for many years." The Holocite stared back. Robbie knew he was serious. "Sar, stop frightening the newbies," came a girl's voice. Footsteps could be heard on the glass floor, short steps, then she appeared from behind the great grey hulk and the voice had a face. She was petite with dazzling blue eyes and long cascading blonde hair. The most beautiful girl Robbie had ever seen. "Hi, I'm Alicia." Robbie didn't speak, he couldn't, he just stood there, mouth agape. "You do have a name don't you?" "Robert" he blurted, even though he hated when people called him that. "So, you're the new guy?" "I guess." Robbie moved to her ear. "Is that why these creatures are here?" Alicia whispered back. "Bit of advice new guy, they don't like being called creatures, they're here because they think you're a big deal. No idea why, Holocites don't talk much, they're more likely to cut your head off and ask questions later." Robbie looked back, panic in his eyes. "Just kidding, jeez." "I've only seen things like that in sci-fi movies" explained Robbie as they moved away from the gathering. "Yeah well, get used to it, you haven't seen anything yet." "What did he mean back there, the grey guy." "Who, Sarugril? I wouldn't pay too much attention to what Sar says, Holocites always speak in riddles. Poor lug hasn't been the same since Oswald died." Robbie looked back at the beast. "I wish I'd known him." "Who?" "My granddad." "Wait a minute," said Alicia taking a step back. "You're

Oswald's grandson? He was a genius, a total hero."

"So I keep hearing." Robbie looked at Alicia and up at the walls around them. "How did you end up here?" "Long story, besides, don't wanna give away all my secrets the first time I meet you now do I? How bout you answer my questions, like how come you've just shown up out of the blue, and please don't make any portal jokes I've heard em all before." "I got a message in my granddad's soul echo, to come here, he said it was important." "Then something big's about to go down. People only leave messages in their soul echoes if they're telling someone they love them or warning them about something, and something tells me Oswald wasn't the mushy type." "You know more about him than I do" said Robbie. "It's kinda my job, I'm a data gatherer. All of the information that comes to us goes through a central Hub computer that's linked to other Circle facilities around the world. We share information, it's my job to see what we need." "Cool" "Not really, but it beats school work. Anyway gotta fly, catch you later Robert." "Rob" said Robbie. "Rob" said Alicia and smiled. "Matheson!" came a roar from a desk behind, "get a move on with those Intel reports!" "See ya" and she was gone.

Chapter Eight

IN YOUR DREAMS

S ally Jones hated rats. It stemmed back to when she was a baby. She could remember one evening as she lay in her pram, the silence being broken by the sound of tiny scurrying feet, her pram lowering as if a weight had suddenly been attached. She could remember seeing the vile black creature making its way over the edge and onto her fluffy pink blanket. It just sat there, with those eyes, beady little black slits with the faintest trace of yellow in them. Unable to speak she lay petrified, tears rolling down her cheeks waiting for the terrible moment to pass. It crept a little, stopped, crept a little further, stopped. Then flicked river water from its wet body and left dragging its thick wet tail over her face. She never recovered from it. It was Sally's worst nightmare. She was the one who had conjured up the army of two hundred black rats outside her terraced home on Applegate Street. Across the street Tom Kress sat up in bed terrified of the creature that lurked in his wardrobe. The creature with the long scaly legs and even longer arms that could snatch him out of his bed if he ever closed his eyes to sleep. Anna Noble had always had a paralysing fear of snakes so when she entered her bedroom and saw the walls contort and twist into different slithering shapes she knew that her nightmare had become real. Though it wasn't until she heard the flash of fangs and saw the serpents make their way onto the landing that she knew she was in real trouble.

But it wasn't just children that were affected by the Dream Streamer, as one snooty old lady soon discovered. Gretchen Oldham dressed her pet in ridiculous clothes, like dog-sized sailor outfits with little hats and scarves. To her, sniffles was the most important thing in the world. "Sniffles, where aw you dawling? Sniffles, come now, don't be a bad doggy, mummy wants you." She called and called but there was no trace of sniffles. Just dead silence. In darkness she made her way toward her garden shed. It sat guarded by two spooky looking oak trees. Usually Sniffles came bounding out from behind the door, his fluffy tail twitching excitedly. Not this time. Gretchen gathered her pink dressing gown around her and proceeded. A low rumble came from inside the shed. "Sniffles?" She got on her tippy toes and peered through the dusty window. In the corner there was something strange rising and falling like a living breathing stack of rocks, it seemed alive, but not. A head emerged from the darkness and two demonic eyes stared back. She ran through the garden in fright, her curlers bouncing out of her hair. Suddenly the shed exploded sending shards of wood flying into the air. Bits rained down around her as she lay hunched down in the grass, rigid and petrified. Nervously she turned back. Standing in the remains of the shed was a behemoth, a vision from hell. A hound with red demon eyes. It had white fluff around the corners of its mouth.

"Sniffles!"

Peter Havisham looked out his bedroom window onto Applegate Street. The lights in each of the houses were out. There was smoke and debris everywhere. "The Dream Streamer" he whispered to himself. Emily entered the room, having gone to check on the children.

"Robbie's gone!"

Peter closed his eyes and did something which he hadn't done for a long time, he used his abilities. Telepathy was difficult to control as it was, but it was made more so by the visions around him, they were obscuring his thoughts. "I think I've got him."

The Cadillac lay parked outside. Peter turned the keys in the ignition, the engine roared to life, it took off through the gates of Havisham Hall and down

Applegate Street. When he reached the city it was full of tall dark figures with death white faces. They gazed in shop windows, eyes rolling feverishly in their heads, their long thin fingers pawing at the glass. Gangs of circus clowns with fat bloated stomachs and sharp yellow teeth rode bicycles made of bone. Peter zipped along the road, his thoughts overcome with a dark presence. The inside of the Cadillac was covered in dials, speedometers, temperature controls, drinks dispensers, and a radar, programmed to pick up just about anything. He punched in a few numbers and a monitor dropped from the roof. He could see from the blue blips that kept flashing that he was surrounded by nightmares in every direction. The blips grew closer. *They* grew closer. He tried using his abilities again, but it was no good.

RAAAAARGH

The scream pierced him like a knife. Peter slotted the monitor back into position. "You wanna play dirty, let's play dirty." Peter dialled in some numbers on the dashboard. A gauge began to fill beneath the steering wheel, one bar at a time. The grotesque nightmares approached, each one more terrifying than the last.

Three bars to go.

Sprites attached themselves to the windscreen and started cutting their way in with long blade like fingers.

Two bars to go.

Larger nightmares appeared and reached under the Cadillac, attempting to snap it in two. One of the sprites was close to getting in, if that happened he was finished.

One bar.

"Come on, come on!"

Screeech! Screeech! Screeeeech!

Peter could feel the Cadillac rising from the road.

Screeech Screeech Screeeeeech!

It all came down to one little bar, that was the difference between life and death.

RAAAAARGH!

The sweetest thing Peter ever heard suddenly sounded in the Cadillac.

Lightning charge activated.

"Gotcha!"

Peter flipped a switch. A blast of light shot from the Cadillac blinding the nightmares. They squealed in pain as the light burned them. The Cadillac fell to the road with a thud. Peter slammed his foot to the floor and rammed them out of the way. Some nightmares tried to follow, but they were much too slow. The city had come to a halt, beasts clambered over car roofs and bonnets. Vehicles swerved to avoid each other and crashed into store fronts. Nightmares began demolishing everything they could find. Turning over cars, uprooting lampposts, smashing shop windows, anything to scare people. Crowds fled through the streets, the horrible visions close behind them. The sound of car horns and screams filled the air. Peter headed for Barber's science supplies. The nightmares marauded the streets. Now *they* were in control.

A siren started up on the corridors of Circle HQ. Red flashing lights dropped from the ceiling. "Alert, alert" came a female voice over the loudspeakers. "This is not a drill. Paranormal activity reported in the city." Everyone on the corridor shot each other terrified looks. Samuel suddenly emerged through a portal and clanked his way across the floor to meet Robbie. "Samuel, what's going on?" Everyone fell silent. Then, as if from nowhere, a tall grim looking man appeared in a grey pin striped suit. He cut through the crowd like a knife, everyone moved aside. Half way down the corridor he stopped and turned, everyone slowly gathered in around him. "Who's that?" asked Robbie. "That's Lombardi" Samuel whispered. Finally the name had a face. Lombardi was a haggard looking man with wiry grey hair. Robbie remembered Oswald's message and distrusted him immediately. He was dressed immaculately and had a pair of spectacles that sat propped over his bulbous nose, and he was old and pale, but had a powerful presence, something told Robbie that he was a lot tougher than he looked. "As you have just heard there have been a number of sightings of paranormal activity. It appears that a band of creatures have launched an attack on the city." "What are we dealing with here Professor?" asked Gordon Bryson from the crowd. "At the moment Mr Bryson, it is difficult to say, I can say however that I have never seen the likes in all my years." Robbie could tell from the way that everyone fell silent and listened to Lombardi that they respected him. Lombardi turned and took a remote control from his pocket. "These images have just come into Hub database." He clicked a button. On the far end of the corridor an LED screen came down from the ceiling and switched on. Suddenly there were images of people screaming and running, the camera was fuzzy but two beings could be seen. One was tall and skinny and dark and had a long flapping tongue that rolled onto its bony chest, the other was fat, grotesque, a cloud of green vapour rolled around it. Robbie could almost smell it from the safety of the corridor. He recognised them both, they were Lucy's nightmares. A shiver ran the length of Robbie's spine. He knew that the Dream Streamer was responsible. Samuel leaned down and whispered. "We have to get you out of here, your father is waiting at the entrance." "My Dad!" "Sssshh, I'll explain later, right now you need to go."

The Cadillac shot out of an alley and careered across the road swerving and sliding at speed. Robbie gazed at the expressionless creatures as they rolled past. They swerved to avoid one. "What are these things?" asked Peter. "Nightmares," said Robbie "they're Lucy's nightmares." "By the way, regards running away from the house, we'll talk about that later." Robbie didn't care. Right now his dad was the least of his worries.

THUMP

A nightmare gripped the hood of the car and inched its way closer. A layer of goo lay across its hateful face, a newborn. More ran out from the side streets and leaped onto the back. "Rob, do your thing." Robbie raised his right hand into the air, charging it up. The nightmare leaped forward. Blue sparks fizzled around Robbie's fist and it shot forward.

SMASH

The windscreen cracked outwards and the nightmare was launched back down the street. Peter shot a look. "Collateral damage" said Robbie turning in his seat. There was a bump and crunch as the Cadillac rolled over its body. Two more clambered over the back seats. Their faces weren't vacant anymore, they were growling, hissing, showing their teeth. Robbie raised his right hand, but this time was different, there was something wrong. The nightmares came closer. "Rob, what are you waiting for?" "It, it won't work." "Rob, hurry." Peter caught their leering faces in the middle mirror. "Hang on!" "What?"

SCREEEEEEEEECH!

The breaks slammed hard. The nightmares were launched forward, flew overhead and cracked with a hard crunch onto the road. The Cadillac zoomed past. "Phew, that was close, what happened back there?" "I got..." "What is it?" "I guess I got scared" said Robbie. Peter glanced over. "That makes two of us." Robbie looked behind, they weren't dead, they were standing, staring, just out of the game for a while.

The Cadillac shot through the gates of Havisham Hall and came to a loud crunching halt on the gravel outside. Robbie hopped out and looked up at the thick black smoke still billowing from the attic window. Peter stepped from the car and picked up a shard of glass that had been blown out by the blast. In a flash of light he was sent back to before the explosion. He could see it all, Lucy going to the Dream Streamer, the activation switch being turned, darkness, then the heat and roar from the explosion. He dropped the shard and walked up the stone steps to the front door. Robbie followed, keeping an eye on the smoke floating out above.

BOOM

He turned around. People on Applegate Street ran from their homes in panic.

BOOM BOOM BOOM

Robbie ran to the gates and looked down into the city, flashes were going off and more explosions rocked the ground. Sirens filled the air. One large building in the centre of London suddenly began to plummet down, as if in slow motion, then a grey cloud of smoke swept out around it. The people at the end of the street let out cries of shock. Robbie's heart beat with fear. It was a sign, a warning, it was chaos, and it was just beginning.

Chapter Nine

SIBLING RIVALRY

Robbie stared across the table at his sister, anger rising. She looked like Lucy spoke like Lucy, but it wasn't Lucy, he'd watched enough horror films to know that, besides, she was far too nice. "The Dream Streamer, it's done something to you." "Don't try to think Robbie, it doesn't suit you." "I'm not afraid of you" said Robbie, even though he was trembling inside. "Well, what a change, little Robbie Havisham finally standing up for himself. You're pathetic, always were afraid of your own shadow." Robbie knew he wasn't speaking to Lucy then, she was bad, but not that bad. He was speaking to something else, something evil. He got up from his seat and went for the door. "Going somewhere?" Robbie didn't look back. Emily and Peter were standing in the hallway, backs turned to the door. Emily turned around to speak as Robbie entered the hall.

"Why would your sister do this?"

"She's not my sister."

"Look Robbie this is no time for arguments."

"No, I mean she's not Lucy."

"What?"

"Whoever it is in there, it's not Lucy."

"Robert my nerves are shredded now just..."

"Hold on a second," said Peter "show me what you mean Rob."

"Peter, you're not seriously."

"Just hold on a second."

Peter followed Robbie into the kitchen. "Hey dad" said Lucy cheerily. Peter had his back turned to her. She gave Robbie a sly look, knowing that she couldn't be seen. Peter cut to the chase. "Who are you?" "What are you talking about, I'm your daughter." Peter stared at her and tried to tap into her mind, it was no use.

"I have a question for you. What did I buy you for your sixth birthday?" There was a long unsettling silence. Robbie could see the thing searching for the right answer, it didn't seem capable of accessing her memories. "Um...a doll" she replied finally. Peter and Robbie glanced to each other.

"Yeah right!"

Lucy sprang from her chair and launched two fire balls down the room. "Dad, look out!" Robbie sent a shockwave that pushed him to safety. "Stay down!" Robbie blew his fringe out of his eyes and started towards her. She fired two more over the table that smashed against the wall. "Things are about to heat up!" she mocked. Robbie raised his right hand. Wind swept the kitchen and knocked her back across the floor. She sprang back, catlike to her feet. "Play nice brother." Robbie launched a collection of plates and saucers that smashed against the kitchen door. A wall of flame shot across the table. Robbie crouched down and looked across at Peter who was sheltered behind a dresser. "Dad, I'll keep her busy, you try tapping into her mind again!" "Good thinking son!" Robbie could see Lucy's shoes under the table. He put out his hand and launched another shockwave. She was slammed hard against the kitchen door and slouched down on the floor.

"Dad, now!"

Peter closed his eyes and found himself inside Lucy's brain. It was dark, tormented, but he could feel the real Lucy behind the dark thoughts, behind the demon attacking them. "Lucy, listen to me, you're ill, something's happened to you." "Dad, what's wrong with me?" "Just stay calm, I'm going to help you." The darkness began to creep back, clouding Peter's mind. Lucy's eyes opened and she rose from the ground. Her body lit up in flames as she walked toward her brother. "You always said I was a hot head, I'm just proving you right." Robbie lifted the kitchen table with his abilities and launched it towards her. She ducked out of the way and smiled. "Lucy, stay away, I don't want to hurt you!" "You're going to kill your own sister?" Robbie stepped back "I knew you'd be too afraid to do what needed to be done." Lucy reached out her flaming hand, as though she was about to fire again. It was right, he couldn't do it, he couldn't hurt her. Robbie shut his eyes and waited for the flames.

"Goodbye brother."

WHACK

Then he opened them again. Lucy lay on the floor in a heap. Emily stood over her with a rolling pin. "Ok, I'm convinced."

Emily stared out the kitchen window at all of the flashes appearing around the city. "It's getting worse out there." She looked at Lucy, still unconscious and slumped against the wall. "What are we going to do? We can't just lock her up." "Until we find out what's going on that's exactly what we're gonna do" said Peter. "What about those things out there?" Peter stayed quiet. He didn't have any answer for this. "I'm going out" decided Robbie. "No way, it's far too dangerous" insisted Emily. "It's my fault. I should have stopped her from going up there." "It's nobody's fault but mine" said Peter. There was silence for a moment. "Peter, what are you saying?" "I knew about the Dream Streamer, I knew it was up there, I've always known." "But, why didn't you say something, why didn't you tell us." "I thought I could finish it, I thought that I could make him proud. I thought that if I made it work the nightmares would go away, mine and Robbie's." Peter turned around, "It's not your fault Rob. Rob? He's done it again."

Robbie ran down the hill as fast as he could. He ran and ran until his legs felt like painful pillars of stone, until his stomach ached, until sweat covered his face and his head spun round and round, then he ran some more. Something that thing said struck a chord. He wouldn't let it win, he couldn't. All of his life he was afraid of the genius gene, of his abilities, of how people would never accept him because of them, but he couldn't be afraid anymore, not this time, this was the line in the sand, a brand new start. He kept his head down, clutched Oswald's soul echo tightly, and headed for the plumes of smoke in the distance.

Chapter Ten

THE HUB

Robbie knew he couldn't confront the nightmares alone, he needed help. He needed Oswald. "Granddad. They're loose." "What is it Robert child, what are you saying?" "The nightmares, Lucy's and everyone's on Applegate Street. Their nightmares are real." "You mean?" "The Dream Streamer, it exploded." "Good God. How could I have let this happen? Listen to me Robert. Go to the Circle, you'll be safe there. Lombardi will have the answers. Go, quickly." Robbie shut Oswald's soul echo. He remembered the materialiser that Samuel Barber had given him. He clicked the button at the top of the device. Two grey portal guardians appeared on the street and stretched out an entrance with their bony little fingers. Robbie went inside the portal and was enveloped in its blue energy waves, safe. For a while everything was blue and calm and tranquil. Wave after wave swept past as though he was in some kind of soothing tunnel.

WHACK

Robbie slammed against a dark wall of books. He picked himself up from a dusty black and white floor and let out a cough. He'd been here before. "Haw haw, young Havisham, I was wondering when you'd be back, I see you've mastered the materialiser, well, almost. I knew an unfortunate soul who ended up stuck in the side of a building once." "Samuel, I need your help" said Robbie, panic in his voice. "Of course, what's the matter, besides nightmares running round frightening the wits out of everyone that is?" "I need to go down there." "Down where?" "Back to the Circle, it's the only way we can stop them." "Are you sure of this young Havisham?" "No, but it's all I've got to go on." "Well, then, after you." Samuel gestured toward the bookcase. "Actually, I kinda wanna do this myself." "By all means. I trust you know where you're going down there?" "Yup... I remember pretty much everything." "Clever clogs eh, you really are a Havisham. Oh and Robert, be careful down there, your grandfather trusted me to take care of you. I don't want you to go hurting yourself." "Can't promise anything!" said Robbie running down the stone steps behind the bookcase. "Just like Oswald" said Samuel to himself. Robbie darted for the intelligence centre where he'd first met Alicia Matheson. He walked past a sign which had several directions on it, among them were the temporal chamber, the money spider lair and the Vashterra temple. He glanced around for a human face, but there was only a sea of creatures behind their monitors. One stuck his head up from the screens and nodded. Robbie gave a quick nod back and quickened pace. In the middle of a group of typing Holocites he spotted her. She was sitting by a computer. "So, the big deal returns" she said swivelling round in her seat.

"I need your help" said Robbie crouching down to talk. "Sure, what's up?" "I need access to the Circle database." "That's pretty impossible, you'd need Lombardi's access codes." "How can I get them?" "Ha, um you can't, unless." "What?" "Wait a sec" Alicia waited for a Holocite to pass by her cubicle. "Come with me." She rose from her chair and walked down the aisle of computers. "If anyone asks, you never saw what you're about to see." Robbie saw Holocites at their screens whisper to each other. "Still a bit of a celebrity down here" said Alicia, barely audible over the chatter in the offices. "Where are we going?" "The Hub, it stores every case file in the HQ, you should find what you're looking for there." Robbie followed her down a long metallic corridor. The floor was steel plated and high up on the walls there were holograms displaying an image of a man with a pale face. He had scars down his cheeks and he had dead black eyes. The most frightening man Robbie had ever seen. Alicia glanced up and immediately looked back down again, as though he might catch her looking. "That's Shellon Mace. Not the kinda guy you wanna run into, but I guess the scars and demented expression kinda gave that away. Well, here we are!" Alicia came to a grubby green wall at the end of the corridor and stopped, "What, this manky wall, this is the Hub?" "Patience newbie." Alicia crouched down and spoke into a radiator. "Activation code Pegasus, Matheson Alicia." The wall shimmered and distorted, Alicia stood away. The wall faded and turned into a huge metallic chamber door. "Holograms, gotta love em." Alicia slipped a card through the metal slot sticking out from the right hand side.

BEEP BEEP BEEP

"Score, we're in." "Wasn't that the plan?" "My cards been outta date for ages."

"Top class security then." "Funny. Come on." She led the way inside.

CHUG CHUG CHUG

The lights came on one by one. "Welcome to the Hub." Inside, a blue light pervaded the room, but didn't manage to reach the corners. One of those rooms where you can't help but feel like someone's standing in the shadows, watching you. In the middle there were lines and lines of computers. There was no sound but the low hum from their processors. "Hey, which..." "Shush!" snapped Alicia as the chamber door closed. "Could you make any more noise, we're not supposed to be in here remember." "Which computer stores the Intel data?" whispered Robbie. Alicia gestured toward a giant screen in the corner. The width of the screen almost took up the end of the room. It looked more like a cinema screen than a monitor. Robbie made his way over to the wall where all around the monitor there were little screens showing camera footage from different parts of the city, others were showing live feeds from the CCTV cameras on the HQ's corridors. "You can probably tell what I had for breakfast" said Robbie. "We can." Robbie just looked at her. "Kidding... what were you looking for anyway?" "Search for anything to do with my granddad and a Dream Streamer." Alicia typed the words Oswald and Dream Streamer into the computer and hit the search button.

SEARCHING, SEARCHING.

O Results found.

"Try Oswald Havisham and nightmares." Alicia put in the search. 6 Billion files found. "Well that narrows it down. Ok, I've got something." Oswald Havisham, the world's leading scientific expert finds new miracle cure for baldness. It was a nightmare trying to find a cure for my baldness, but finally Mr Havisham has done it... "Not exactly what you were looking for then?" "Not exactly." "There must be some way to get the info, but only your granddad would know how. He hooked this stuff up." "Who told you that?" "The Professor, they were pretty close. Sarugril would probably know how to get into it too, he was your granddad's defender." "Defender?" "Oh God" sighed Alicia. "I forgot I'm gonna have to explain every little thing to you." "Ok, each member of the Circle has a Holocite bodyguard, they're called defenders. Sometimes it's too dangerous for humans to go on missions alone so Holocites protect us. Sarugril is the strongest and oldest Holocite there is, that's why he was assigned to protect your granddad. I'm not supposed to tell you this, but Sarugril is next in line to be your defen... "

VWOOORP

A screen lit up under Alicia. There was a picture of a boy on her console. "Who's that?" said Robbie. Alicia hit the quit button. "Doesn't matter. Find anything?" Robbie was suspicious, but he went along with it anyway. "Not a lot, some of the entries have been deleted." "Wait, that can't be right." Alicia scooched into the seat under Robbie's chin and started typing. After a moment she sat back, a puzzled expression on her face.

"You're right. But that doesn't make any sense. Who'd do something like that? All of the information here is supposed to be preserved." "Not anymore, can I try something?" asked Robbie. "Sure, knock yourself out" Alicia rolled her seat out of the way. Robbie clicked and typed and opened windows here and there, so fast that Alicia could hardly keep track of them. "Ah, there's our problem." "What's our problem?" "It's encrypted, we need to bypass the security locks by overriding the protocols here in the Hub." "How do you know this stuff?" "Fast learner." "Wait" said Alicia "it says here that this information was deleted two days ago." "So... they're probably clearing out space." "No, you don't understand, the only people who are able to access this information are your granddad and Professor Lombardi. I know Lombardi would never touch it." "So what are you saying, someone wanted to cover something up?" "I don't know, but something doesn't feel right." The sound of footsteps could be heard on the corridor outside. "Hurry, someone's coming." Robbie noticed a folder on the desktop. Oswald Havisham family file. The steps drew closer. "Get a move on Robbie." Robbie looked at the chamber door and hesitated, then reached for the mouse and clicked to open the file. When the file opened it was a family tree connecting every Havisham going back to Jeremiah, he searched for his own profile on the screen. "Hurry!" The chamber locks began to release. "Robbie get out of here. Now!" Robbie reached into his pocket and clicked his materialiser. A portal opened, he jumped through.

CLICK

The chamber door opened, two security guards entered. "Matheson, what are you doing in here?" "Just reviewing some old cases" said Alicia flushed. A look of suspicion crept across their faces. "Well, get a move on, we're in an emergency here, we need everyone on intel." Alicia slunk out under the guards and checked

Robbie's location on her scanner. He'd returned to Samuel's shop. Alicia walked down the steel clad corridor trying not to look at the images of Shellon Mace, the Circle's enemy number one, the destroyer of worlds, the bringer of death, the dark one. She worked alongside people whose families he had killed, it wasn't easy for them to see his leering face everywhere. She never knew what to say to them, except that he'd be brought to justice, and even she didn't believe that. She shuddered and prayed that she'd never have to meet him in person. A hand appeared from nowhere and firmly placed itself on Alicia's right shoulder. "Not so fast" came a female voice. Alicia turned around knowing she was busted. Before her stood Ziva Vaugier. "Circle internal affairs" said Ziva showing her badge. Ziva was around twenty five years of age. A French Circle agent whose job it was to spy on her fellow workers. For the safety and transparency of the institution she was told, but it didn't make her job any more pleasant, and it didn't make people trust her any more, especially since it was well known that Ziva was half vampire. "Back from Paris then?" "Yes, the situation was... contained, the threat eliminated." "In other words you won?" "I always win" said Ziva whipping back her long dark hair and folding it back inside the collar of her long leather jacket. "My business is here now, Lombardi told me we are in the middle of, how do you English say... state of emergency?" "What gave it away, everyone running around like headless chickens or the monsters tearing the city apart." "A little of both" said Ziva with a slight smile. Then her expression changed, as if she suddenly remembered to be serious. "What were you doing in there anyway, and don't lie, I can always sniff out liars." It was true, she had a vampire's senses, she could see a heartbeat from miles away and smell sweat just as easily. "Robbie wanted to look up some old files on his granddad" said Alicia. "Ah oui, Robert Havisham. The grandson of Oswald no?"

"Yeah. Why do you French people always say no when you mean yes?" "Be careful around him Alicia, he is more important than you realise, Lombardi wants him protected at all costs." "That's all anyone ever thinks about isn't it, who's important and who isn't." "Alicia" "Alright alright, I'm not a kid you know." "You are ten." "Fair enough. How'd you know he was here anyway?" "It's my job to know these things. Samuel Barber was also very helpful in providing me with information." "That weirdo. Doesn't he have better things to do? Like clean the cobwebs out of his crummy little shop." "This is a serious matter Alicia. Robert could be the key to finding out what's going on. He may also hold the key to much more."

"Like what?"

"Sorry, but that is classified."

"Well, how long are you gonna be nosing around?"

"That is classified."

"Do you think one of us is responsible for all of this?"

Ziva didn't answer. "Let me guess, classified?" "Exactment!" "Well if you wanna start investigating things maybe you should check why half of Oswald's files are missing." Ziva looked puzzled. "Someone deleted them two days after he died. I told Robbie that only his granddad and Lombardi had access, Lombardi wouldn't delete them, would he?" Ziva turned on her heels and said aloud. "If there is one thing I have learned Alicia, it is that everyone is a suspect."

Chapter Eleven

THE CASE BEGINS

Ziva Vaugier began her investigation immediately. There was no time to waste. Professor Lombardi was powerless to stop her from questioning who ever she wanted to. The first person she needed to speak to was the last person who had seen Oswald alive, none other than Samuel Barber. "Ah, Miss Vaugier, what can I do for you this time old girl?" "If that is another vampire joke it is not funny, besides, I didn't think Centaborgs were known for their sense of humour." "Ah haw, you must not know many Centaborgs then." "I am on official Circle business. I have been hired by London branch to look into our current situation. My senses tell me that what is happening is somehow linked to Oswald Havisham." "Oh, I see." "Would it be possible to ask you some questions?" "Why yes, of course." Samuel clanked his way across the black and white tiles of his shop and cleared away the junk that had stored up for months on a nearby table. "Please, sit." "I will stand merci." "Very well." The giant stabilisers in Samuel's mechanical legs lowered to the ground, allowing him to sit comfortably by the table. "Well then, how can I help you?" "Monsieur Barber you claim to have been with Oswald on the day of his death, can you describe that day to me?" "Well, yes of course, it was a Friday. Oswald appeared very excited that he had reached a milestone in his latest experiment. One could always tell when he was excited about something you see because he had the peculiar habit of straightening his tie, and pacing back and forth, he was a world class pacer." "So he was physically fit? "Fit? He could run rings round just about anyone, and that's saying a lot. Even poor Sarugril had trouble keeping up with him." "Would you say then that it was strange for him to die so suddenly, of a heart attack?" Samuel looked puzzled. "Miss Vaugier, are you trying to suggest that Oswald *didn't* die of a heart attack?" Ziva smiled "not at all monsieur Barber, it was just a question." "You're not hinting at foul play are you? No one here would be capable of such a deed, surely?" "Please, it was just a question. Tell me more about that day." "Well...it was quite normal really, not many people entered the shop because there wasn't much activity below. It had been a quiet week on the paranormal front I suppose, if he only knew then what was coming." Samuel's head lulled forward as if he had just become depressed. "Monsieur Barber, is it OK to continue?" "Yes, yes, I just... well, to be honest, I just can't believe he's gone. We were the best of friends you see. In a way Oswald was the man who rescued me. Life wasn't easy for Centaborgs many years ago. Very few people know this, but I grew up on an air force base, just outside of Winchester. The authorities didn't quite know what to do with us back then. In a way I can't blame them. Centaborgs are an unusual species, even by human standards. They had set up a wing especially for us, and decided to keep us on base, many of us flourished, but many were kept as... as pets, for the troops amusement. Oswald was the man who achieved equal rights for *all* Centaborgs. He brought us to the Circle, gave us jobs and opportunities. He was the most decent man I have ever known." "You told me before about his grandson, Robert." "Yes, a brilliant child. Oswald would talk about him endlessly. He had great hopes for him. He could never contact him however, he was always afraid of the risks attached to combining work and family, God knows it can be dangerous." "It must have been hard on the boy, growing up, knowing that he had a grandfather who he could never see." "I would imagine so. It's not fair that only some of us had the pleasure of knowing him." "Robert has his grandfather's soul echo," said Ziva "that should be of some comfort to him." "True, true." "In fact," said Ziva "that brings me to another question. I met Alicia Matheson recently, she told me that some of the data that Oswald stored in the Hub had been deleted. Have you any idea of how that happened?"

"Deleted? But, that's impossible, why would he delete his own files?" "He didn't. The files were deleted two days after his death." "But that would leave, Lombardi?" "I will come to Lombardi later. Right now I need to speak to some of your co-workers." "Is there any way we can retrieve the files?" asked Samuel. "Doubtful" said Ziva. "Indeed, it would take Oswald himself to figure this one out." "Him, or a relative" replied Ziva "Thank you for your time monsieur Barber. I will speak to you again soon I am sure." Samuel nodded and Ziva disappeared into the darkness of his shop.

Chapter Twelve

PHOENIX RISING

"Peter, Peter, she's coming round" said Emily from the edge of Lucy's bed. Lucy opened her eyes as Peter entered the room. "Mum, where am I?" "You're at home darling, you had a....well, maybe your father can explain." Peter sat on the bed. "It was my fault dad wasn't it? I went up there. I wouldn't listen. Robbie tried to stop me." "Shush, that doesn't matter now, try to get some rest." "Is Robbie ok?" Peter looked to Emily. "I honestly don't know." Lucy struggled in her bed, Emily and Peter had been left with no option but to tie her down for her own safety, and theirs. Sweat rolled down Lucy's face. "I can feel their fear dad. I'm scared." "Me too Lucy, me too, but we're going to find a way out of this, I promise. Get some rest now." Peter got up from the bed and joined Emily by the window. "Will she be alright?" asked Emily. "I'm able to read her thoughts for the moment, but they're getting clouded, whatever was controlling her is starting to come back." Emily looked at her daughter with a terrible expression of grief, her eyes widened in sudden realisation. "Peter, with Robbie gone, if she decides to burn up, we won't be able to stop her." "I'm dangerous mum aren't I?" said Lucy from the bed. Neither Peter nor Emily spoke, they just looked to each other. "I knew the genius gene would make me do this." "That's not the problem Luce," said Peter "it's not you. Something happened to you, when you used the Dream Streamer." "Peter we've got to do something!" "We just need more time" said Peter concentrating on Lucy. "We haven't got more time!" Peter looked at Lucy and shuddered, he knew she was right. Emily looked out the window and could see the nightmares hovering in the sky above. More were appearing every minute. Lucy's eyes started to flicker and a pale blue colour appeared in them. "What's happening?" asked Emily. Peter stayed silent, hoping for the best, but that wasn't good enough, not now. Lucy's eyes opened. "Lucy. Lucy darling, we're here." "Lucy isn't here anymore" replied a deep demonic voice. "Emily, step back!" The curtains above Lucy's headboard caught fire, her arm restraints sizzled away. Lucy rose from the bed, a trail of fire around her. "Peter, do something!" "Your tricks will do no good here Havisham. I only want the boy." "It's talking about Robbie, Peter stop it." Peter shut his eyes and tried to stop her, it was useless, the creature's mind was blank, dark with hatred. He stood in her doorway, blocking the exit. "No more mind games" said the thing inhabiting Lucy's body. She flung a jet of flame that shot out like a snake and nipped at Peter's face. She fired again, Peter hit the floor. He was powerless. Lucy calmly stepped out over him and left.

Suddenly the great wide doors of Havisham Hall burst open and Lucy walked out. Out on the streets there was no sign of the turmoil going on in the city. She walked down the hill in flames. "Time to set this town alight."

Ziva Vaugier walked the corridors of Circle HQ. She had questioned some Algarons from the higher levels, been to see Sarugril and now needed to speak to Robbie. Ziva could tell that a friendship was growing between him and Alicia. A friendship that could be useful to her investigation. She turned the corner and walked onto a corridor that led to the Circle's botanical gardens. As she approached she could see Robbie and Alicia standing outside.

"So, this is Robert Havisham, bonjour Robbie, comment allez vous?" "tres bien merci, et vous?" "oui, tres bien." "What the hell are you two talking about, and since when do you speak french?" said Alicia turning to Robbie. "Genius remember?" "Yeah, wonder how I keep forgetting that." "Robert, I need your help" said Ziva "Sure." "Can you recover your grandfather's data from the Hub?" "I can try." "Excellent, I was hoping that your reputation was well deserved." "I didn't know I had a reputation." "For all that you know Robert there are still some things that you don't. Please, lead the way." Robbie was surprised that anyone was asking him to do anything, he'd begun to feel like a tourist around the Circle. Robbie, Alicia and Ziva came to the unassuming radiator that became the chamber door into the Hub. "Activation code Pegasus, Matheson Alicia." The chamber door emerged before them. "You humans and your holograms" said Ziva stepping inside. "Robert, can you show me where the information was stored?" Robbie went to the computer where he'd seen the files and started typing away. He was incredibly fast. Ziva looked at Alicia. "I know, don't get me started." "Ok, I think I've found something." "Very good, what does it say?" "I've got the schematics of the Dream Streamer. Whoever deleted this information must have known about it, and they probably knew where my granddad stored it." "That means that the data was deleted by someone close to Oswald" said Ziva. "Well aren't you a regular Sherlock Holmes?

What else does it say Rob?" asked Alicia. Robbie was looking at a screen that read...

IN CASE OF EMERGENCY

"Em, I think we might be in serious trouble." "More serious than we're already in?" said Alicia. "Well, actually, yeah."

From the stone corridor leading to the central committee chamber Professor Lombardi could hear the gathering of Circle members discuss the effects of the Dream Streamer. He looked haggard as he took the stand to address his fellow members. "Gentlemen, gentlemen, silence, please." The mumbling began to subside. "We are gathered here to discuss recent events. A night in which the nightmares of one hundred children came to life and stalked the streets of London. A night in which a man who has not existed for more than one hundred years was spotted walking the streets of Whitechapel. A night in which an army of zombies marched down Oxford street." Lombardi paused for a moment, inhaling deeply. "A night in which the rules and guidelines of this institution were brazenly disregarded. Let us remember gentlemen that we each took an oath, to advance the field of science, to protect the citizens of London, and most importantly, to never let the two come into conflict. We stand here as men of science, to find a solution to this problem and to end this catastrophe before it escalates any further." Lombardi could hear a faint cough from one of the stalls above him. He recognised it instantly. "Do you have anything to add Mr Humble?" William Humble rose shakily to his feet. He was a short man with curly brown hair and a kind harmless appearance. "Actually pr, pr, professor I do" he said, wiping a bead of sweat from his brow. "Well, go on." "When, when you said before it escalates any further Professor, I, I'm afraid that it already has." Lombardi's face drained of colour and sank into his chest. "How do you mean Mr Humble?"

The mumbling began to rise again. "Well Professor, based on information which I have just received from our friend Ziva. It appears that the things we've been seeing up to now are, somewhat isolated cases, in that nearly all are children's nightmares." "Yes, yes," said Lombardi frustrated "what of it?" "Professor, Robert Havisham has helped Ziva to retrieve data which had been deleted from the Hub. In that information Oswald Havisham had warned that if such an incident occurred, it would be as a result of sabotage." Audible gasps were heard around the assembly. "And... according to this data, every day that these nightmares walk among us, the more plentiful they will become. You see Professor, they appear to feed off of our fear. It is their food source." Once again the assembly burst into chatter. "You mean?" "Yes Professor. The more afraid people are, the more nightmares there will be."

Chapter Thirteen

PARK FIGHT

Alicia tracked Robbie to the conference centre on the lower levels. "Having a little snoop around are we?" Robbie was slouched down in a comfy red arm chair, tinkering with the materialiser that Samuel had given him. "There's only one reason someone deleted that stuff" said Robbie, "they were hiding something." "I know" said Alicia, "but who, and why?" "That's what I'm gonna find out." The materialiser in Robbie's hand lit up. "Robbie, how are you doing that?" Alicia had never seen a materialiser work that way before. It emitted a low blue light, just like a portal opening, but there *was* no portal. "I'm not, not really," said Robbie "I re-wired all of the components in this materialiser so that it can send me to where Lucy is." "How do you come up with this stuff?" "I don't know, I guess I just figure it out." Alicia stared in amazement. It had only taken Robbie a few hours to crack technology that some members of the Circle *still* hadn't come to grips with. Robbie took the location device from his trouser pocket and jammed it into the side of the materialiser. It sent out a beeping sound from the mini screen, the co-ordinates on the screen were pointing toward Kensington Gardens in Hyde Park. "Rob, are you sure you wanna do this, fight her I mean." "I don't have a choice, I need to stop her." "Well, I'm coming with you, as much as I can't stand your constant questions I..." "What?" "I don't want you to get hurt." There was a little uncomfortable silence.

"Thanks."

"...Alright, let's get this done."

Robbie pressed the button at the top of the materialiser. A bright blue flash appeared. Suddenly Robbie and Alicia appeared through the portal and landed on the outskirts of Hyde Park. Alicia looked around.

"No creatures here then."

"Don't speak too soon, I hear something."

The growls of nightmares started in the distance. They could smell Robbie and Alicia from miles away. "They're coming." "Look, Rob, I'm not a genius, but I know you're keeping things to yourself. Where'd those things really come from?" "You really wanna know?" Alicia nodded.

Robbie told the entire story, he could hardly believe it himself, he could hardly believe the situation that he'd been plunged into, and for the first time he knew why he had never met Oswald. He understood what his granddad was protecting him from.

"Let me get this straight, your granddad created a machine that could destroy nightmares, but when your sister went inside it she became possessed, and released her nightmares into the city?" "Not just hers," corrected Robbie "the entire neighbourhood's." "You're not really normal, are you?" "Not really." "Don't sweat it.

My family are the weirdest people I know." "Trust me, mine are weirder. Wait, stay down." There was a band of nightmares ahead, savagely attacking each other and screaming into the cold night air. Then Lucy emerged. Robbie's heart tightened, something told him that this was round two. Lucy stood between two wrecked cars, flames engulfing her, behind the inferno the nightmares lurked. They gathered around her, her pets. Nothing could be seen through the fire but her bright possessed eyes and her jet black hair, and nothing could be heard but the crackling of heat and the nightmares' growls. "Who the hell is that?" said Alicia in awe and fear. "She's my sister" said Robbie, a lump in his throat. "I take it back, your family *are* weirder than mine." "Come on," said Robbie "we've got to get out of here." They fled through the park, huddled down behind a dark green bush and peeked over the top. "Looks like they're patrolling the place" said Alicia. "Or guarding *her*" Robbie replied. "We're not gonna be able to take her alone" said Alicia. "Whatever the plan is you'd better do it quickly." Alicia took out her materialiser and punched in the code on her handset. "What are you doing?"

"Sending for reinforcements."

WHHHIIIIRRRR

A blue light flashed in the park. Sarugril appeared through the portal. "Humans, what are you doing down there?" "Trying not to get killed" said Robbie. "Good one" remarked Alicia. "Thanks."

Sarugril looked up at Lucy and the horde of nightmares. "We've got an infestation. Stay down." Sarugril crunched his knuckles and started toward them. The nightmares sniffed the air, they knew something had changed. Lucy turned and nodded, sending them into battle. "Who's first?" One nightmare shot forward. Sarugril swung.

WHACK

The nightmare launched into the air smashed through the tree branches above and landed onto the grass with a crunch. "One down." More closed in fast. One slammed into Sarugril, pushing him through the grass. Sarugril's hooves ripped the soil apart under him as the nightmare held on. They were locked in a battle of strength. Sarugril let out a toothy smile and launched his knee up into the nightmares chest. A snapping sound echoed around the park. "He's good."

"That's nothing."

Robbie could only imagine what she meant. He'd never seen anything so fast or so vicious. "Next" roared Sarugril. Two more dropped from the trees. One dodged left, the other right, Sarugril grabbed both by their necks. "Going somewhere?"

SMASH

Their heads clunked together and they fell onto the grass. Sarugril whipped round quickly, three nightmares ran straight for him. He leaped high into the air and landed on a thick tree branch above. The nightmares climbed the giant oak like spiders made of bone and scraps of flesh. "You things just don't give up, do you?" One darted forward almost shoving him over the edge. "Oh, no, you DON'T"

SLAM

Sarugril punched the nightmare over the side. It smashed a park bench below. Two more were waiting for him. "This is going to be easy." Sarugril dropped from the branch, landed on the grass and reached for his utility satchel. He took out an electro whip and cracked it toward the tree. The strong sizzling whip wrapped itself around the giant oak and seared into the wood, cutting through it like a hot knife through butter. The nightmares looked on stupidly as the tree leaned to one side and finally snapped. They clung on as it plummeted to the ground and crushed them under its heavy body. "Impressive," said the demon. Sarugril turned and saw Lucy, or at least her body.

She was smiling, a huge nightmare stood protecting her. "Permission to take down the girl" asked Sarugril through his head set. Robbie shook his head. "Negative," said Alicia "don't touch her." "I can take them both." "No, I said don't touch her, she's..." "She's what?" "She's Robbie's sister." "Sister?" "You heard what I said, now don't attack." Robbie looked over the bush and could see Sarugril backing off. "I need to do something!" "Robbie don't! She's too powerful!" Robbie knew she was right, but he had to do something, he had to try. He stood up. "Robbie, what are you doing? Get down!" Lucy sensed his presence and lit up in flames, her nightmare bodyguard and Sarugril stood back, they knew this wasn't their battle. "Nice of you to join us Robbie, I was wondering when you'd start to fight your own battles." Alicia looked on from behind the bush. "Sarugril, keep an eye on him, don't let that thing touch him, sister or not, if she attacks so do you." Sarugril nodded. "You couldn't hurt your sister back in that mansion, and you can't hurt her now, you are too weak." Robbie didn't listen, he just walked towards her. "I'm not afraid." "I can *feel* your fear Havisham. The fear that's consumed you all of your life, the fear of being different, of being a freak." "You can talk" whispered Alicia from the bushes. "Fear makes you weak, and it makes us strong. You long to be normal, but you can never change the blood coursing through your veins. I can set you free. I can kill you here and now, or...you can join us and pledge allegiance to Lord Mace." Alicia's heart leaped. "Did she just say Mace?" "Affirmative" replied Sarugril through gritted teeth. "Permission to attack?" Alicia looked on, wrestling with the decision. "Wait." "I will give you two minutes to decide." "I don't need one" replied Robbie. "I was hoping you'd say that." A wave of fire cut through the park scorching everything in its path. Robbie blocked the blast with an energy wave. His right hand shot out and Lucy was knocked against her nightmare bodyguard. Alicia peeked over the bush, her mouth agape. "Why didn't you tell me he could do that?" Sarugril stood back, his arms crossed over his broad chest. "Come on Robbie, you can do it." "Nice trick," commented the demon rising to its feet "but I've got some of my own." Fire ripped along the grass almost catching Robbie's feet. He hung still above the raging inferno, struggling to keep himself in the air. Lucy turned and nodded to her bodyguard. The colossal beast grabbed a nearby tree, crunched it in two and flung it at Robbie. He ducked and landed on a safe patch of grass. Sarugril stepped forward. "Let's do this together Robbie, you focus on your sister, I'll take down the big guy." Robbie nodded, Sarugril charged. The nightmare bodyguard stomped forward. Sarugil reached for his utility satchel and flung two smoke grenades into the beast's path, he hung back for a moment. "Do it Robbie, do it now." Robbie fired an energy wave at the trees behind Lucy. "You can't kill me boy!" The trees plummeted down but just as they were about to crush her a protective ball of flame emerged around her, vaporising the falling trees. "All you can do is give up." Robbie was exhausted, using the genius gene was like tensing a muscle, he couldn't keep it going forever. "You are tired, weak. And now you are going to die. GET HIM!"

A horde of nightmares took off like dogs let loose from their leads. Sarugril clenched his grey fist and slammed it into the first one he saw. More scattered from behind Lucy. There were dozens of them now, coming from everywhere. "We gave you a choice and you threw it away!" cried the demon into the night. Wave after wave of fire blasted the park, kicking up clay and scorching everything. "Kill the boy, bring his body to me!" Robbie dodged the flames and hovered away. The nightmares were focused, they wouldn't stop this time. Robbie's energy failed him and he stopped again. He stood rooted to the spot with fear. There were too many of them, he couldn't stop them all. He tried to run but his legs betrayed him. "Robbie!" shouted Alicia "get out of there!" It was no use, Robbie had the same feeling that he had back in the Cadillac, as if his best wouldn't be good enough.

SLASH

A nightmare clown swiped at Robbie's face. More crowded him. A hulk emerged through the jeering and filthy mob and swung a vicious punch into Robbie's solar plexus. He was knocked back across the park and slammed hard against a beech tree. Winded he fell to the ground and struggled to keep his eyes open, it was no use. Sarugril reached his limp body just as his eyes closed. "Sar, get him out of here!" Sarugril turned towards Lucy and her nightmare bodyguard.

"This isn't over."

Chapter Fourteen

THE INFIRMARY

R obbie's eyes flickered and opened. He strained at the bright glare of what he thought was the sun. His pupils took a few moments to adjust, a few moments to take in his surroundings. He felt the ground with his hand, but instead of feeling grass he felt a soft cushiony fabric. He was in a bed and the sun above was a cold sterile medical light that reached out over it. He blocked his eyes from the glare and focused on the blurry figure sitting on the edge of his bed, it was none other than Professor Lombardi. "You took quite the nasty knock Mr Havisham. I don't believe we've been formally introduced. My name is Professor Lorenz Lombardi. I run everything you see around you." Robbie tried to speak, but he was too weak. "I believe you came here to learn more about Oswald, indeed if you were not his grandson you wouldn't have gotten past the entrance. I don't know what Barber was thinking. Oswald was very much like you Robbie, always willing to get himself hurt for the greater good, and look how *he* ended up. All you need know about your grandfather is that he was a good man, and whatever is happening out there he is not responsible... no, it was someone connected to Mace." It was the third time Robbie had heard the name but it didn't hold a scrap of meaning for him. "Oswald would turn in his grave if he could see you now. He spent his entire life trying to protect you from the forces of darkness and within a week you come face to face with an infiltrator." It was the first time Robbie heard the name of what had possessed Lucy. "You have no idea of the dangers out there Robbie and you are definitely not equipped to confront them, not yet." Robbie sat up. "What are they? Infiltrators I mean." "Infiltrators are the minions of Mace. They use people's bodies as vessels to stir fear, to sow seeds of doubt and deception. This infiltrator was obviously sent to cause this disaster and soften our defences." "Professor, who *is* Shellon Mace?" "Shellon Mace is known in Holocite folklore as the bringer of death, the end of all things. The one who will boil our oceans and scorch the earth, he will raise the forces of darkness and destroy every living thing on the planet. Mace has no grand plans, no desire to rule, he only wishes to destroy life, every form of life." "Why would he want to?" "Does madness need a reason? Shellon Mace is the product of the worst evil imaginable. In 1990 the Circle discovered a portal between our world and the next. It was designed to explore the possibilities of dimensional time travel, but the powers that be didn't account for one thing." "What's that?" "A door swings both ways." "Mace got through?" "He arrived with a dark army. The losses were catastrophic, but the Circle managed to force them back through the portal. Many humans, Holocites, and Centaborgs, died that day. The Circle thought they had seen the last of him, but in the last few years we've seen an energy signature spring up in different parts of the world, outside of our institution's portals. It appears that Mace is trying to break his way into our world once more. So far our defences have held, but it is only a matter of time before he returns. "What happens if he does?" Lombardi didn't speak, he just sat on the edge of the bed, his eyes downcast, for the first time he looked just like a weak old man. "Mace has many agents that can creep into our dimension through pockets called time rips" he said changing the subject. "The one you experienced out there is an infiltrator. "So you're telling me this Mace guy sent something to possess Lucy?" "Listen closely" interjected Lombardi "is there anything your sister has done recently, anything unusual?" "The Dream Streamer" whispered Robbie. "What did you say?" "My granddad, he invented a machine called a Dream Streamer. It was a machine that could destroy nightmares, or at least it was supposed to." "Blast you and your secrets Oswald!" Robbie turned his head and could see Sarugril and Alicia out on the corridor. "I have already spoken with your new friends and mark my words they will face severe punishment. They had no right to bring you into this." "I'm already in this!" "That you are Robert, and I fear you don't understand how bad a place it is to be." Lombardi took off his spectacles and wiped them with a pristine white handkerchief. "Get some rest. Something tells me we'll all need a little over the next few days." Lombardi rose from Robbie's bed and gestured for someone to enter the room. A low humming noise started up and Lombardi left. Shiny blue medical robots entered, carrying trays of food, fixing Robbie's pillows, and even bringing fresh flowers to his bedside. Robbie glanced across at a tray of medical equipment that had syringes, scalpels and a small bottle of disinfectant laid out on it, thankfully none of his injuries had been that bad. Robbie looked up at a series of framed holographic projections that hung high on the walls around his bed. All of the people in the frames had cuts and bruises on their faces. To his surprise Oswald was among them. Robbie darted up in his bed but a sharp pain stabbed at his back and he lay back down. "Eh, hi" he called to one of the robots, or medbots as the Circle referred to them. "Excuse me" he called again. "HELL O!" The medbot wasn't listening, when it turned to tuck in Robbie's blankets Robbie could see that the metal panel over where its stomach should be read ZX 20. "ZX 20?" The medbot suddenly shot to life. "Yes sir, how may I be of service?" "Why are those holograms up there, who are those people?" "They are the school of hard knocks sir." "What's that?" "The school of hard knocks is a phrase coined by David S. Maracovey to describe people who have frequented the infirmary on a regular basis. The robot spoke like, well, like a robot. "Can I help you with any further questions Robert Havisham?" "What kind of injuries did my granddad have?" "Please specify." "What kind of injuries did Oswald Havisham sustain while he worked here?" The robot stood upright, as if processing the information. "April 23rd 1953 concussion, July 9th 1954 fractured ribs, August 25th 1954 broken wrist, the list went on and on. "What was his last injury?" "Oswald Havisham's last recorded appearance in Circle infirmary was on November 23ʳᵈ 2011, admitted as a result of poisoning." Robbie's heart skipped a beat. "Poisoning... but that can't...who checked him in?" "Oswald Havisham checked himself into Circle infirmary." The medbot called out statistics on Oswald, on the day in question but Robbie didn't listen to the rest, he'd heard enough. "Will there be anything else sir?" "No, that's it..." he said to the air. Robbie lay back, looking at the animated holograms in the frames above his bed. He knew one thing was for certain, Oswald hadn't died of a heart attack. He'd been murdered.

Chapter Fifteen

ZIVA, WARRIOR PRINCESS

Ziva Vaugier stood in the bathroom of her quarters, filing down her teeth with a sharp blade. There was nothing worse than a vampire who didn't care for personal hygiene she always thought, and anyone who knew anything about vampires knew that the teeth were the most important part.

Knock knock

"Who is it?"

"It's Robbie. I need to speak with you."

"One moment please."

Ziva placed the blade down onto the counter by her sink and wrapped her nightgown around her. She opened the door to her quarters. "Can I help you Robert?" "What are you doing about the missing data?" "I am sorry, but that information is classified" "I don't wanna hear it, this is my granddad we're talking about!" "Please, come in." Robbie walked inside, his head was bandaged up and he had a slight limp after the force at which he was knocked to the ground, but he didn't care about himself, there were bigger things at stake. "I want to know why you're here and what you're doing about the data in the Hub." "Well, if you must know I have conducted interviews throughout the day, so far I have spoken to half a dozen Holocites, including Sarugril, a few Centaborgs, many members of the Vashterra community, and some Algarons from the higher levels." "What about Lombardi, he runs the place, *he* must know something." "I have not been able to interview him so far." "I want him interviewed, I want something done" demanded Robbie. "Robert, why don't you tell me why you are really here." "My grandfather," managed Robbie, his lip quivering with emotion "...someone, someone murdered him... and when I find him." Ziva stared at Robbie, fully acknowledging the gravity of the situation. "Mon Dieu, please, Robert, sit down." Robbie sat by Ziva's coffee table. "Why do you say these things?" "I asked the medbot in the infirmary about his injuries, it said he'd been poisoned." "Poison?" said Ziva bringing a hand to her chin, but, that can't be true." Robbie hung his head low, as if the events of the last few days had suddenly taken their toll. "Robert, I know this is very difficult for you, but if you are sure of this information then we must learn more." "What do you want me to do? I didn't ask for any of this...he told me to come here!" "Robert, you came here to learn about your grandfather, to learn about the man he was, that has not changed." Robbie said nothing, he just sat with his head down. Ziva moved from her position on the seat opposite and sat down beside him. "I have never told this to anyone, but Oswald was very special to me too...he saved my life you see." Robbie calmed a little. "It was during the Vampire Wars. Oswald was a young man at the time, though obviously I have not aged. It was a vicious battle, we had been overrun ten to one, they had attacked in huge numbers and caught us by surprise. Your grandfather always kept cool under pressure, he never let them see the fear that he felt. One of the vampires, a cruel and heartless beast called Vola attacked me from behind, stabbing me with his katana blade, he vanished soon after, like the coward he is. I had been badly hurt. Your grandfather carried me to safety and healed my wounds. He told me that I would survive, that I would live to fight another day, and that the Circle was proud to have me on its side. Before that day I never trusted humans, but when I was dying, defenceless, your grandfather showed me the best of humanity, he showed me why the Circle needs to exist, to protect our human species. "But, you're half vampire." "I am also half human" Ziva replied with a smile. "I want Lombardi questioned," said Robbie "I want you to promise." Ziva put a hand on Robbie's shoulder. "Whoever killed your grandfather will pay, *that's* a promise."

Emily reached into the attic and felt nothing but ash. She climbed up and saw that the whole floor lay covered in a thin layer of it. All of Oswald's experiments were semi-submerged, like a black snow had fallen on them. She dragged her pale blue dress up into the attic after her, which was now covered in dirty black smudge marks. Emily walked the length of the laboratory, her pale blue dress flowing through the ash as she passed the vials, test tubes and once gurgling bits of apparatus. "I remember this" she said picking up a strange looking metal sphere with spider like legs sticking out of the bottom. It was Oswald's Vortex 52 prototype, a spy device that he was building for the Circle. Emily made her way around a large counter near the centre of the room. On the floor sat something that she hadn't seen for many years. A wooden chest. The words Oswald Havisham were inscribed on it. She lifted the lid.

Inside, there were old newspaper clippings and articles. She took one from the box, clutching the badly aged paper. She read...

Oswald Havisham, a man of the future

Sir Oswald Havisham, inventor, surgeon, entrepreneur. There are no limits to the man his peers call "The Master." Having graduated in medicine from Oxford University Oswald went on to finish a P.H.D at Cambridge, before entering the field of science. This is where he found his true calling. Having accumulated numerous awards the brilliant boffin seems unstoppable. As well as being the inventor of the Neuroliser, a device used by surgeons the world over. Havisham's multi-billion pound company goes from strength to strength. The truly inspiring part being that all of this was achieved before his fifteenth birthday. Mr Havisham now lives in West London with his wife Beatrice and son Peter who already shows signs of his father's genius having recently finished first in a national science fair.

Emily placed the tattered article inside the pocket of her blue dress. She knew how much it would mean to Peter. She still couldn't believe that it had only been a few days since Oswald's death. She walked to the window. Below, at the black railings that surrounded Havisham Hall, stood the old woman. Emily's heart froze, she could barely breathe. The old woman seemed ill, she coughed into her handkerchief and was deathly pale, she looked up, saw Emily, and began to move away. Emily dashed from the window and out onto the corridor, she needed to speak to her, she needed some kind of explanation. Emily ran as quickly as possible, down the corridor, down the next set of stairs and the next one and the next one and the next one. Finally the stairs that led to the bottom floor came into view. Surely she'd have enough time to catch her? She bounded down the red carpet and onto the black and white tiles then pulled with all her might at the gigantic wooden doors that led outside. Emily ran down the pebble path that led to the railings. She looked up the street and down, the woman had vanished. Emily stood panicked, out of breath, and quite alone. Everything seemed so quiet, eerily peaceful. The autumn leaves helicoptered to the ground and added to the piles which had gathered on the pathway outside.

Chapter Sixteen

SO FAR SO BAD

All of London was gripped by fear. It didn't take long for people to take matters into their own hands. Mobs took to the streets brandishing all sorts of weapons, none of which were effective against the hordes of nightmares. Newspaper vendors flailed copies of the London Times screeching "Hell on Earth!" and "The end is here!" The major landmarks had all been overrun: Big Ben, Trafalgar Square, The Houses of Parliament. Even the Thames had become home to nightmares that resided in water, they built their nests along the banks where their young were free to flourish and grow. The Prime Minister was at a loss to explain the creatures, as were the police. Most officers had abandoned their stations and retreated into a panic along with everybody else. In a matter of hours the thin fabric that holds society together had unravelled and everything had descended into chaos.

Lucy and her nightmare army now controlled the streets unopposed. She smiled, taking in the fear of the people that hid in their homes, who felt powerless. She delighted in it, it was her power source, her food, and the more scared people became, the stronger she felt. Winged creatures with giant tusks scanned the city for victims. Spider like nightmares scurried along through the city's alleys setting up webs and searching for people to cocoon. The larger nightmares were the worst, they were the ones that did the most damage. Crashing through police barricades they swept through the streets, attacking anyone they could find. They knocked squad cars into shop windows and crunched them against buildings. Papers swept the down the deserted streets that were once so busy with shoppers. People used to go to work, they lived their lives. The nightmares had changed all of that. Lucy signalled for her pets to stop, there were hundreds of them. Every one stopped at her command. She stood on the empty road, her black dress flapping in the wind. The nightmares huddled around her, waiting for instructions. Her eyes blazed with hatred. There was no trace of Lucy Havisham now, just the infiltrator that Shellon Mace had sent to destroy London, to destroy the Circle. Snakes curled around Lucy's feet as she brought a flaming hand to the air. She pointed to a building across the street. Over the massive door a large golden sign read HAVISHAM INDUSTRIES.

"Bring it down!"

Robbie sat in the Circle's canteen, reading a file on his granddad. Alicia entered. "Hey, I've been looking all over for you. They do the best hot chocolate I've ever tasted in this place," she said sliding into a seat across from him "Holocites love the stuff." Robbie stayed silent and barely acknowledged her presence.

"What's up with you?" Robbie blew his dark fringe out of his eyes. "Ziva didn't tell you?" "No, she didn't say anything. What's up?" "My granddad" Robbie had trouble saying the words. "Someone... killed him." "Oh my God, Robbie... Robbie I'm so sorry." "I should have been stronger, I should have been able to stop her." "Robbie, no one *can* right now, that's why you're here. We need you." "She used to say that I was scared of everything... maybe she was right, maybe my granddad died for nothing, whatever he wanted me to come here for, maybe I'm just not good enough." "You fought her, you faced her, she's still out there, but that took courage! Don't sit here feeling sorry for yourself, there are people out there that need your help, including Lucy!" Robbie stayed silent, he knew she was right, but he wasn't ready to admit it just yet. "You know, there's one thing you never told me" said Robbie. "You never told me why *you* came here. I told you *my* reason but you never told me yours." "Yeah, so?" "When we were in the Hub, a picture of someone came up on your screen, a boy, you switched it off and acted like nothing had happened, you didn't even tell me who he was..." "Nothing gets past you does it?" "Nope," said Robbie with a slight smile. Alicia shuffled in her seat. She didn't want to tell him, but she owed him that much. "It happened years ago... my brother and I always went exploring in the woods near our house. One day, pretty far into the woods Max found a hatch that led underground, it had been left open. He wanted to go down, I told him not to, that it was dangerous, but he didn't listen and went anyway. I stayed on the surface, I was too scared to follow him. I called and called but he didn't reply. After a few minutes I went in. It was cold and dark down there and the smell was disgusting, all I saw around me were wet dirty walls and a river of waste that flowed along to a lower level. I followed it, calling Max's name, he still didn't answer. I got scared and went to turn back.

When I did the ground beneath me gave way and I fell for what seemed like forever, the fall knocked me out. I woke up in the infirmary. Professor Lombardi had found me and brought me here, he saved my life. I asked him if he had found Max too, but he hadn't. We set up search parties but Max had vanished. Lombardi told me that I should go home, but I've never given up trying to find Max, I know he's still alive, I know I can find him." "I'm sorry..." "It's ok, it's not your fault. We'll get through this together Rob, all of us. That's what the Circle is all about. No matter how weird or different you think you are you'll always have a place here." "I'll help you to find him." "Thanks Rob." Alicia could tell that Robbie was exhausted. His energy had been sapped since his confrontation with the infiltrator. "I wonder why he wanted me to come here, my granddad I mean."

"I have a pretty good idea."

"You do?"

"We've got to keep this between us Rob. No one can know where we're going."

"Have I ever let you down?"

"Frequently."

"Seriously, who am I gonna tell? I need to know Alicia. For him."

"Ok... follow me."

Chapter Seventeen

The Holocite Scrolls

*T*his place is desolate, the air freezing, the earth but a blackened crust which once sustained life. But there is a new life form in this place. A conqueror, and this planet is his trophy. He sits upon a throne of bones. His guards and followers surround him. His name is Shellon Mace and he murdered this planet and its 15 Billion inhabitants. Burnt trees bent and crooked kneel before him, as though defeated and beaten down. His macabre throne stands monstrously tall. Metal fences protrude through the dead soil around it, like a gaping mouth poised and ready to devour anyone who steps too close.

"Show me the girl" said Mace from his throne of bones. A heavily built and grotesque guard placed a pearl coloured globe before his master. "The girl is in

the human city of London Lord Mace." Mace looked into the ball and could see Lucy walking the streets, crowds fleeing in terror.

"The plan is working, the humans are scared."

"And what of our spy, what news of him?"

"He is safe my Lord."

"I did not ask of his safety!"

"The plan has worked my Lord, Oswald Havisham is dead."

"Then nothing stands in my way."

"There is another Lord Mace. A boy."

"A boy?"

"It appears that Oswald kept him secret, protected him from us."

Mace stood up from his seat, he wore a long black robe that draped over his white leathery skin. His eyes were little black orbs and his teeth were filed to sharp points. "I want this... boy, removed." "But Lord Mace, we must wait until another time rip appears."

"My patience has come to an end with you minion."
Mace turned as fast as lightning and sunk his sharp
filed down teeth into the guard's neck. Black blood
spurted from the victim's neck. Mace looked like a
lion hunched over the body of a fallen deer. He bit into
the guard's neck several more times before he rose up
from the corpse and wiped the blood from his mouth
with the sleeve of his robes. "You! Remove this" he
said to another petrified guard. Mace walked down a
stone path that led down from his throne of bones. At
a lower level there were prisoners that he had stored
away. They were all stacked together and gasped for
air through the metal bars of their prison cages. The
prisoners weren't human, or Holocite, but Centaborg.
"Remind me again why I keep these useless specimens
alive." "For your ingenious plan Lord Mace" said one
of Mace's more snivelling sycophants. "I am perfectly
aware of why they are here you imbecile, get out of
my sight!" The impish creature scurried along and

disappeared. Mace looked up at his body guards. "To the rest of you... Kill the boy!"

The top ranking members of the Circle gathered in the committee chamber to hear Professor Lombardi. The Professor took to the stand. "Ladies and Gentlemen, may I please have your attention. As you are more than aware we have been attempting to end the current reign of terror. I am delighted to announce that, to combat the nightmare threat we have assembled a Dream Squad, with the sole purpose of eliminating these creatures before they cause any more havoc." The gathering burst into thunderous applause. "Our Dream Squad are a highly trained group who have run many simulation missions. We have also learned from our hours of research that there are many types of nightmares, these are just a few. Lombardi motioned for the lights to be switched off in the chamber. The lights went out and a projection of the nightmares shone up on the wall. "This is a soul reaper" said

Lombardi. "They have bodies similar to bats. They have a gigantic wingspan and have been spotted gathering people up. Some have already fallen victim to them, where they bring the bodies we have no idea. Many have been spotted in the skies above Carnaby Street." Lombardi clicked for the next projection. "These are night walkers. They have spider-like bodies and can crawl at terrifying speed toward their prey. These appear to be the foot soldiers in the infiltrator's army. Then there are the clowns, who I must admit frighten even me. They have long sharp claws, sharp teeth and apparently smell revolting. There are of course many, many more, however these appear to be some of the *girl's* nightmares, so we will target them first. Now, without further ado I would like to introduce my ace in the hole, my pride and joy, my Dream Squad." Lombardi motioned for them to join him on stage. "Gordon Bryson. Military expert." Gordon Bryson was a strong-looking man with broad shoulders and a stern-looking expression under his furrowed brows. "Natalie Stockton. Nightmare analyst." Natalie took to the stage, took off her spectacles and bowed to the crowd. "Reginald Perrywinkle. Paranormal consultant and engineer." Reginald came next, a nervous-looking man who felt uncomfortable in the spotlight. "Mr William Humble. Data analyst, consultant, librarian and medbot technician." William came to the front of the stage took a half bow then scurried to join the others at the side of the stage. "Mr Gabriel Wollerslock. Foot soldier. Technician. Engineer." Wollerslock walked right across the stage and joined the others, not even bothering to look at the crowd. "Samuel Barber. Entrance keeper, security advisor, portal overseer." Samuel clanked his way across the stage.

CLANK CLANK CLANK

Then took a brief bow that made him almost topple into the crowd. "and finally," said Professor Lombardi "ms Ziva Vaugier!" The crowd seemed shocked, whispers could be heard everywhere. Even the Dream Squad seemed stunned, they had no idea that she'd been selected. "Ziva Vaugier" repeated Lombardi "Circle internal affairs. Foot soldier. Vampire expert and nurse." The whispers continued, and the Dream Squad suddenly began to look very nervous. "I want to say that despite our... no, I want to say that *because* of our differences, we are strong. I am very, very proud of our branch. I believe with all my heart that it is the very best in the world. I want you all to know that we will get through this *together*. I want to wish our Dream Squad luck, and hope that they will come home to us safely. We *will* succeed. I believe this!" One person in the crowd began to clap, followed by another, another person stood and began to clap, suddenly the crowd burst into applause. The lights came on and Lombardi walked off stage. "I believe Professor" said a nearby Holocite. "Thank you" said Lombardi. "I believe in Robert Havisham." Lombardi looked surprised.

"The Holocites are a proud and noble species," said Lombardi "I hope you are correct." "We need not hope anymore Professor, he is here among us. This battle will not be won by you or I, but by the boy. He is the one Professor, he is the key."

Robbie and Alicia walked up through a perspex tunnel that went way up into the higher levels like an escalator. There were signs on the way.

Shooting Gallery, Armoury, Recreation Lounge, Temporal Chamber.

Robbie and Alicia turned a corner and went to a nearby elevator. It was entirely made of glass. Robbie and Alicia took the elevator down to the lower levels. Each floor of the Circle passed by in an instant and disappeared. After a few moments the elevator finally came to a stop. Alicia stepped out, Robbie followed. The floor wasn't a floor at all, but a rocky ground, more like the caves that Robbie and Samuel had crossed to get to the Circle. "What are we doing down here?" "Be patient newbie, everything will be explained." "That's what you always say." "That's 'cause it's always true." Alicia led the way down a long stoney passageway. Its walls were old and brittle and looked like they might collapse at any moment, ancient and cold and full of dark secrets. Robbie thought of how different the place looked from the futuristic style of the Intel Centre and the main building. On the walls there were lit torches. "They've been burning here for as long as anyone can remember," said Alicia. "They were supposed to have been put here by the Vashterra, but I don't believe that." "The Vashterra?" "The original undergrounders, the creatures that discovered these caves. They were here before even the Holocites, they thought that the world would end because of the return of a dark spirit. They thought he'd cast a spell that would block out the sun for a thousand years."

"Mace."

"That's what some think, there are hundreds of interpretations. The Holocites are obsessed with these scroll things, they're sacred. To them this is a holy site, we shouldn't even be down here. Come on, follow me." Slivers of light came in between the cracks in the ancient stonework. The walls looked like they could just crumble away like cheese. Robbie ran his fingers along them and golden dust sprinkled onto the ground. Robbie and Alicia entered a central chamber and Robbie looked up. There was a giant stone column in the centre of the temple that had thousands of transparent boxes stored in it. They reached high up into the vaulted ceiling and disappeared into obscurity. Robbie moved closer and took one into his hands. There was a piece of perfectly preserved parchment inside. Robbie knew from the writing that it was thousands of years old. Golden light flowed into the chamber like sunlight, but he knew there was no sunlight miles beneath London. Something else was creating that light, something powerful. "What is this place?" he asked looking in awe at the column. "It's where the scrolls are stored, the Holocite scrolls." Robbie walked around the majestic pillar, his eyes upraised at the amazing site before him. "The legend goes that the Holocites stored scrolls under the city to keep for future generations, they believed that the war against the dark one could only be won with the help of a warrior named Valrik. The Circle site was built around it. It holds..." "AHEM" came a deep voice from the back of the room. Sarugril stepped out from the shadow of the rock above him. "You should not have brought him here, not yet." "If not now, when?" retorted Alicia. Robbie looked at them both, their eyes were locked on each other. "Stop talking about me as if I'm not even here!" This got their attention. "Does someone wanna explain what's going on?" Sarugril turned to Alicia. "Leave us" he grunted. Alicia knew she had to leave. She turned and gave Robbie a gentle smile, and then her expression changed to the look that girls get before they start crying and she walked back up the tunnel and disappeared. "You shouldn't have said that to her." "She should not have brought you here, it is not time." "Time? Time for what, I don't know what you're talking about, all you ever do is speak in riddles, how am I supposed to know what's going on if you never tell me?" Sarugril stroked his strong grey chin and gave Robbie a long look. "Perhaps you are right." "Great, yeah, I am, now tell me what's going on!" Sarugril looked up at the shining column and at the glyphs etched into it. "This stone tells an ancient story Robbie, a story that is important to every living thing. Humans, Holocites, Norkons, Vashterra, every species in the Circle, every species in the world" "What is it?" "The Holocite scrolls are documentation of a prophecy made millennia ago. The prophecy of hope. It stated that the world will be saved by a boy. A boy with a special gift, among his fellow humans he will become a god. We will be saved by blood which

carries great power." "The genius gene." "Precisely."
"You think Mace is coming back, don't you?" "We
are simply biding our time until Mace returns. The
Circle cannot stop him. But I am hoping, in time, that
you can." "But what can *I* do, I'm no leader, I'm just
a kid." "On this, you are wrong. If the prophecy is
correct you are so much more." "Even if you're right,
what if I don't want to be a leader?" "If you do not,
our cause is hopeless, our war lost, our fate sealed."
Sarugril crouched down and pointed to a line that ran
down the centre of the glyph. "This line symbolises
the blood of the one who will end the war." "Look, I
didn't wanna get mixed up in any of this!" interrupted
Robbie fiercely. "I wouldn't be here if it wasn't for my
stupid sister." "It was your own curiosity that brought
you here Robbie, about Oswald, about the Circle." "I
wish I'd never found his soul echo. I wish he'd never
died." There was silence for a moment. Robbie looked
at the golden sand beneath his feet. He felt like never

raising his head again. Sarugril moved to his side. "You can carry on his memory Robbie, by being brave, for your sister, for your family. I know you never knew Oswald, but *I* did, and I know that he would be proud of you." Sarugril sat down in the sand beside Robbie. "The most important thing isn't being the leader. The most important thing is to be brave, to stand up for what you know is right when nobody else will, even if it means that you will be hurt or mocked or shunned, to weather the storm. This was Oswald's wish for you Robbie, to fulfil your destiny." Robbie looked up at the golden column that housed the Holocite scrolls. "Do you ever feel different from everyone else?" "Every time that I look in the mirror," replied Sarugril "but I wouldn't have it any other way." Sarugril rose to his feet and dusted himself off. "It is our differences which make us strong." Robbie stood up too. "Bit of a cliché isn't it?" "Cliché or not, it is true." A beeper sounded from somewhere inside Sarugril's utility satchel.

"Beepers, I still can't figure them out." A little smile spread across Robbie's face. "It's Lombardi. We're needed at a meeting." "What for?" "I don't know, but when Lombardi calls a meeting it's never a good sign."

The Dream Squad assembled around a large oak table in the briefing room. Bryson, Stockton, Barber, Ziva and Lombardi sat at the top, Robbie and Sarugril sat at the opposite end. "We will attack them before they attack us" announced Stockton proudly. "It does seem the only option" agreed Lombardi. "That's it," scoffed Sarugril "that's your plan. In case you hadn't noticed, those things are ripping the city apart. Isn't it a bit late for a surprise attack?" "We didn't know how they worked earlier, but with our modified weapons they should pose no threat." "No, that's not how they work" explained Robbie. "Professor, really," said Stockton "are we going to listen to the advice of a little boy?" "The little boy is Robbie Havisham, so show some respect" demanded Sarugril ", and you Ziva, why are you joining this insane mission?" Ziva had her eyes downcast. "I thought you were with us?" said Robbie. "I am, but I am also a soldier, I must carry out orders." Gordon Bryson stood forward. "No offence Sarugril, but you have your job, we have ours. Now let us get on with it!" Sarugril turned his attention to Lombardi. "Professor, please, tell them." The Professor looked weary. "We're running out of time Sarugril, we have no choice." "But this is madness, you can't believe this will work. It's a mistake, the boy has been here only a short time and *he* can see it!" "The order has been given Sarugril, what do you expect me to do, my command is at stake here." "With respect Professor, there is more at stake than your job! Good men could die, do you want that on your conscience?" "All I know is that London is being terrorised, and we must put an end to it." "Without the full facts?"

"The decision has been made Sarugril. This meeting is adjourned." The Professor gathered his notes gave Sarugril one last laboured look "I am sorry old friend" and left the room. Robbie went to Ziva's side, she looked disappointed with herself.

"Ziva!"

"Oui?"

"Bon chance"

"Merci Robert, et vous."

Ziva smiled and left. Sarugril slammed his fist through the briefing room table. "He doesn't know what he's doing! This fight can't be won with muscles and bullets. Ziva knows that. Like she said, she's a soldier. We all are now."

Chapter Eighteen

WAY DOWN IN THE HOLE

"What are we doing 'round a manhole cover in the middle of the night?" asked Reginald Perrywinkle, the most nervous of Lombardi's dream squad. "From the Professor's findings many of the nightmares have appeared underground, specifically beneath Oxford Street. Otherwise known as right here." "What do you propose we do?" "I propose we destroy them before they reach the streets." Bryson lifted the manhole cover and waited above ground as the others crept down into the darkness. The ladder was cold and slippery. The first down was Wollerslock, landing in a puddle. He looked around the cracked and wet walls of the sewer. They were surrounded by flowing drains and the city's waste. "They couldn't have picked a nicer place to hide out?" "What were you expecting, a hotel?" "Draw

flashlights" ordered Bryson. "Yeah, that'll scare 'em."
"Do you think the rumours about him are true" said
Newton. "Who?" "Mace, I heard he went mad after an
experiment at HQ." "Are you really on about him again?"
said Bryson. "Well, the whole thing *is* a little strange.
Everyone thinks he's coming back, but no real sightings
anywhere. I think he's made up, like a bogeyman." "Trust
me," said Bryson "he's not made up." "How do *you*
know" said Wollerslock. "I saw his file." "The Professor
gave you Mace's..." "Sssshhh, quieten down, we're here."
"Great, now what?" "We wait."

SWOOOSH

"What was that?" panicked Newton. "What was
what?" "I thought I saw something." "Just calm your
nerves and keep your eyes open, we can't make any
mistakes down here." Bryson took a black device with a
blue screen from under his coat. A low beep came from
it. "What's that thing?" "A spectral scanner. Tracks
paranormal movement from up to thirty five meters.

Werewolves, ghosts, vamps, basically anything that goes bump in the..." "Wait" said Newton. "Where's *our* vamp?" "Ziva!" said Bryson stifling a roar. "Everyone split up, look for her, when you find her contact me, don't approach her, we don't know if we can trust her, not yet." Wollerslock walked down a raised platform beside an open drain where the water dropped down into the gloopy disgusting filth beneath. "Hold on, I'm getting something" said Bryson checking his scanner. A beep rang out, echoing around the walls. "What's that, what does that sound mean?" panicked Newton. "It means they're here." "What do you mean, here?" "All around us." The beeps intensified. "They're close."

BEEP BEEP BEEP

"Very close! Alright everyone, get ready." "Why aren't they showing themselves?" "They know we're here" said Wollerslock. "Where's Vaugier, blast it, where's Vaugier!" "Forget her, we have to move on." "Let's get out of here" said Stockton. Suddenly a greasy looking creature dropped from above and landed in front of them, as if the ceiling had given birth. The team moved back. The nightmare let out a deafening howl, its entire body was covered in a thick slime and its mouth revealed a set of razor sharp incisors. It stomped forward. "How are we supposed to stop that?" "Just stay calm, don't panic." The nightmare stood before them, grotesque and menacing, staring through the Dream Squad as if they were nothing at all. It began to move off. "Reach out to it" Bryson said to Wollerslock. "Reach out to it? Are you mad, it'll take me bloody arm off." "Stop being such a coward!" said Bryson. "I've always been a coward, I'm not gonna stop now." "We don't have time for this!" bellowed Bryson. Samuel stepped out and clanked his way toward the nightmare. "Samuel, don't get too close." "It's quite alright old chap, Lombardi said these ones are harmless." The beast turned its back on them. Samuel could see the muscles in its back rise and fall, and see the hooks that ripped out through its translucent skin. "You're an ugly old bean awn't you?" "It's probably not the best idea to go insulting them" said Newton. Samuel turned around to face her. "Don't worry, they're dumb animals, they don't even know what I'm saying." Suddenly the nightmare whipped around. Samuel was swiped across the sewer and plunged into a river of waste. "Weapons" called Bryson. The nightmare stomped forward. "Fire, fire!" "What is this thing?" screamed Newton. Bryson emptied an entire clip into the beast's chest, still it moved. Stockton pumped four more into it. It gave a deafening howl, blood oozed from its chest and back but it gathered speed and headed for Samuel. "Sam, look out!" Samuel was flung backwards again and crunched hard against the sewer wall. He hit the ground, crumpled. "Sam! Someone see if he's alright!" "It's not interested in us," shouted Stockton "it just wants to reach the streets." "We came here to kill them, not let them go. Reload, take that thing down!" The team reloaded and blasted off a barrage of shots, they pierced the nightmare's skin until huge bits of flesh hung loosely from its body, still it followed. Bryson looked at Samuel, unconscious on the ground. "Alright. Everyone retreat!" Ziva suddenly dropped from the ceiling and stood confronting the nightmare. The beast stared back. Their eyes locked on each other. The nightmare broke eye contact with Ziva suddenly and stood upright. It knew the Dream Squad wanted to escape. It began climbing the steps leading to the manhole cover. "It's blocking us off" shouted Stockton. The nightmare stared down at Samuel's unconscious body. "The rest of you, leave, I will stay with Samuel" said Ziva without emotion. "We can't leave without you" said Bryson. "You can do no good here. I will fight the beast alone." "I guess we should be glad there's a bit of the vamp left in you yet," shouted Bryson "alright everyone, you heard her, let's get out of here." The Dream Squad moved off down the sewer and disappeared from sight. Ziva's eyes shone in the darkness, fangs shot from her mouth, she stood up and crunched her knuckles.

"OK, now it's just you and me!"

Chapter Nineteen

NIGHTMARES ON THE MOVE

The nightmare lunged forward. Ziva reached into her leather jacket and took out her custom made Samurai blade. She swung and caught the nightmare's hand. It fell to the ground. The beast howled in pain. Ziva stood back and stared in amazement as the hand re-grew itself from the nightmare's wrist.

"Interesting."

"RAAAARGH!"

The nightmare lashed out, knocking Ziva off balance. She fell back onto the hard slimy cement floor. "Nobody ruins my clothes!" The beast stood over her, its yellow eyes bulging. She hopped back onto her feet and slashed the nightmare's ankle. Ziva was faster than the nightmare, but she couldn't match it for strength. It picked her up by the legs, she dangled in the air as if she was just a toy.

"Put me down you disgusting thing!"

The beast threw her down the length of the sewer like a piece of unwanted trash. She landed, sliding backwards on her feet, her sword ready to work. Ziva charged and ran under the legs of the nightmare. She launched herself up behind its shoulders and started to land blows across its back. The nightmare didn't even feel them. She sank her fangs into its beefy neck, again the nightmare did nothing, it just jerked forward a little, as though a bee had stung it, and like a bee Ziva was swatted away. She was knocked clear and landed into a pile of waste. She rose from the trash covered in dirty sewer water.

"That's it. Nobody ruins my clothes!"

Ziva's eyes blazed bright white with fury. She stood staring at the grotesque beast that had all but repaired itself after her attacks.

"This is your final warning!"

The beast roared in defiance and sent her hair blowing back. Ziva placed her Samurai sword back inside her long leather jacket. Her nails extended out to ten times their natural length. She ran in a blur of speedy colour and scratched frantically at the creature's legs. It howled and lashed and swung about the place trying to knock her away. She dodged every move.

THUMP

The nightmare fell to the floor, defeated. It lay on the ground, breathing shallow breaths. Ziva would have felt sorry for it if it hadn't come so close to killing her. She turned and started to walk away. She knew exactly just how close it had been, she knew she was lucky to be walking away with her life. She had cuts all over her face and she was drenched in dirty water. She focused on getting back to the Circle and having a warm bath. She thought of Robbie and the colossal task that was ahead of him. She prayed that he really *was* the one that Sarugril had such faith in. All of a sudden the atmosphere in the sewer changed. Ziva sniffed the air, something was wrong. A shadow was cast up over her on the walls. She looked puny in its presence. She turned around and almost fell to the ground in shock. The nightmare had risen to its feet, again. It caught Ziva in its gigantic hand and crunched her against a large cement pillar. Her body went limp, her head lolled forward. The nightmare dropped her to the ground with a sickening crunch. It stepped out over her lifeless body.

Robbie loved puzzles and equations, even though he often solved them in minutes if not seconds. He had a photographic memory that came in useful in all sorts of situations. Now he was tracking down his grandfather's killer. He'd have to employ every trick in the book to find him. This would be his dedication to Oswald, he owed him that much. Robbie sat at a control panel in the Hub, searching thousands of files, cross-referencing information, watching old security tapes. The most important file wasn't on any computer however. It was stored in Robbie's mind. He remembered everything that had happened in the Circle with perfect clarity, every word spoken and everyone who uttered it. He began to piece together who he thought would have reason to kill his granddad and who he thought would keep information from him. He hacked into each personnel file one by one. He checked Lombardi's first.

Professor Lorenz Lombardi

Age: 62

Education: Eton College

Personal History:

Lorenz Lombardi was a bright young student who excelled in the field of science. His first contact with the Circle occurred on the 2nd of May 1982 after a terrible incident at his home in Warwick. Lombardi's wife and children were killed in a ferocious attack, which was later discovered to have been perpetrated by Vampires. Lorenz Lombardi then joined forces with long time friend and industrialist Oswald Havisham to breathe new life into the Circle institution. They updated and ran London branch for many years after.

Robbie had always known that there was something dark about Lombardi's past, something that ate at him. But instead of being arrogant and aloof like Robbie had first thought, he realised instead that Lombardi was in very deep pain. He was a man with a troubled mind. Robbie thought of how many people saw *him* the same way, because they just didn't understand him. "Switch it off" came a voice from the back of the room. "Professor?" "Off, Mr Havisham." Lombardi entered into the light. "If you were a member of the Circle I could have you thrown out for such a breach of trust, as it stands I am simply disappointed, I thought

Peter would have raised you better." Robbie went red and felt embarrassed. "What you saw in that file is none of your business... however... I believe I know why you looked there, you don't trust me, you think I am the one responsible for Oswald's death, but I am not. I promise you this." "Yeah, everyone's his friend, but somebody killed him, somebody in the Circle." "I can understand your frustration." Lombardi seemed genuine so Robbie layed off him, for the moment. "I'm sorry about your family," said Robbie. "It was a long time ago, another life really, but I've never been able to forgive them for what they did." "But, you work with Ziva, she's a vampire." "Half vampire" said Lombardi "besides I have learned to make sacrifices and I have learned that hatred only destroys a person, piece by piece, day by day until there is nothing left at all." "That's kinda the way I feel." "For a long time you will, and you will never forget Oswald, but the pain will pass, as everything does. I think we may have more in common than you realise Robbie Havisham." "There's one thing I don't get, if you and my granddad were such great friends then why would he keep the Dream Streamer from you." Lombardi smiled to himself; your grandfather was a brilliant man, but a reckless one. Oswald designed many machines over the years, some were more successful than others, and some were just plain dangerous, as his friend I felt compelled to tell him when he had created something that could be a hazard. I would imagine the message was just another example of his rebellious nature." "But you didn't come here to tell me *this* did you?" said Robbie. "Alas I did not. I have just received news that the Dream Squad have failed in their mission... Oswald was my friend Robbie, and I know of the faith he had in you. He told me once that you were the key to all of this, to the Circle, to London, to our future. I met a Holocite today who believed the very same thing, in fact, they all do. We're out of options." Lombardi took off his spectacles as if to accentuate his seriousness. "You are our only hope now Robbie." "No pressure then." "Maybe just a little." Robbie smiled. He became serious then, this needed to be. "I've got to find her Professor, to end this." "I understand." Robbie got up from the console he'd been seated at. He walked towards the entrance. "Robbie!" called Lombardi "Be careful out there."

Robbie appeared through a portal to Lucy's last known co-ordinates. He walked down a deserted street searching for a familiar face, for anyone. Ahead he could see the remains of a building that Oswald had built, the very first Havisham Industries factory. It lay smouldering in a pile of rubble. Only the black skeleton of each room stood in the smoke. Everything lay in a layer of thick grey ash. Stepping inside it was obvious that it had been attacked by a nightmare. It bore all the signs. Claw scrapes along the walls, large hoof like footprints in the dust. The attack was more frenzied than any he had seen before.

It was clear that the nightmares had gotten personal, that the infiltrator was trying to send a message, to draw him out, and that's exactly what it had done. Suddenly at the end of the burned out factory Robbie spotted a colossal nightmare. It was Lucy's bodyguard. The beast stomped around the remains of the building like a T-Rex hunting its prey, its vicious yellow eyes searching, scanning, analysing everything. It turned and looked straight at him. Robbie didn't have time to react. Before he knew it the beast was in the air landing punches down on top of him. Robbie was knocked against a charred pillar and he fell onto the ash-covered ground. Lucy's bodyguard burst through a series of wooden construction frames and lumbered forward, its sharp teeth holding back a bucket load of drool. It was ravenous. Without warning it swung its giant powerful fist again. Robbie ducked, avoiding the colossal sight flying toward him. It was angry, very angry. A huge chunk of plaster and concrete began to fall. Spotting the debris Robbie leaped to safety while the bone crushing load crashed down. Dust covered the room and spread out in a massive cloud. He stayed on the ground, the dust made it impossible to see. After a moment he got up. There was no sign of the grotesque scaly beast or any indication that it had survived. Robbie breathed a sigh of relief, which wasn't easy in the swirling dust picked up by the wind. As he walked away he began to think of his family, of the danger they were in. Deep in his thoughts he couldn't have heard the shifting of rubble as a long bony claw made its way to the top. It was only when the ground became dark in shadow that he turned to see the menacing vision of Lucy's bodyguard rise from the pile that it had been buried beneath. It rose slowly, stood still for a moment and darted forward. "What's this thing made of?" Bounding through walls the unstoppable juggernaut hadn't slowed at all; instead it was angrier, stronger. It was close enough now for Robbie to smell its pungent breath. When he turned again there it was. Robbie's heart sank. The creature's dead eyes stayed fixed on him all the time. This is it, the end of the line Robbie thought. He had no choice, he had to fight or die. Robbie turned quickly stuck out his hand. A blast of bright blue light knocked the beast off its feet and back through the remains of the building. It ended up out on the streets. Robbie followed it out of the destroyed structure. He noticed a green light emerge in the nightmare's eyes. It was hypnotic, he looked away, he couldn't allow anything to weaken him, not at this stage. Dark grey clouds rolled across the sky. They let loose a volley of cold raindrops. Robbie stood at the end of the road, Lucy's nightmare bodyguard stood at the other end. The nightmare knew it was dealing with no ordinary human, it was dealing with something more, something else. Puddles began to form in the craters left by the beast's colossal footprints. Robbie looked into one. He gazed at his reflection and knew that whatever happened in the next few moments it would change everything, forever. Up ahead the nightmare was snorting, and scraping the road with its gigantic claws. Robbie breathed in deeply and prepared himself. The nightmare leaped toward him, Robbie rolled out of the way and got to his feet. The nightmare stood close to a billboard, a billboard for Havisham's medical supplies. It lifted the sign from the metal supports that it sat on and fired it across the street. Robbie thought fast. The sign smashed into shards. He barely had time to move before the nightmare came barrelling at him again. Robbie rose into the air above the nightmare and landed behind it. "Behind you! You ugly mutt!" The beast turned. "That's it. This way!" Suddenly the sound of a car's screeching tyres rang out, breaking the nightmare's concentration. It was a family who'd gotten lost in the chaos. They pulled up at the nightmares foot. The driver hid behind the wheel while his wife and children screamed in panic. The nightmare moved toward the car. "Nooo! I'm the one you want. C'mon, fight me!" The beast turned and focused on Robbie. "C'mon!" The beast gazed into the car and sniffed the air, as though it was trying to catch the scent of fear. Robbie fired an energy wave that knocked the nightmare off its feet. The driver took his chance to escape. He backed up the car and reversed down the ruined street. Robbie walked purposefully toward the fallen beast, he knew he could beat it now. The beast got to its feet slowly. Robbie didn't give it the chance to re-gather itself and fired another wave up into its chest. The beast flew through the air and smashed into the 23rd floor of a block of apartments. It shook itself off and roared at the occupants of the room that it had landed in. They sat petrified on their couch. The beast grabbed both sides of the hole that had been created by the impact and launched itself out. Robbie stared from the streets below. The nightmare darted toward the ground its claws outstretched. There was no time to run. Robbie curled himself into a ball and pointed his palm upwards. A giant protective globe encased him in a blue energy shield. The nightmare crashed down onto it.

BOOOOM

It sounded like a thousand claps of thunder rolled into one. The noise burst all of the windows for miles around. Robbie rose from the blue globe and walked toward the nightmare, which lay on its back and was covered in smoke from the power of the collision. It was winded. "Give up." The beast laughed, a loud sadistic laugh. "Why can't you just stay down!" The nightmare leaped to its feet and swung at Robbie. Robbie was launched backwards and landed a few yards down the road. He sat up and coughed out a little blood, then wiped his lip and stood up. His hand charged and fizzled. Blue sparks flew everywhere.

"C'mon!"

Robbie stood, heart-pounding, body shaking. He knew it was *it* or him. The beast took off again. Robbie looked up and saw that great chunks of building were falling away from where the nightmare had crashed into it. They fell and smashed onto the street below. He used his abilities to raise up the chunks and sent them crashing into the side of the weakened nightmare. It stopped and tried to swat away the oncoming debris. Robbie walked forward keeping the chunks flying all the time. A large lump of rock plummeted down and cracked across the nightmares head. Robbie ran over, it was hurt and lay on the road. He was face to face with it now. "LOOK AT ME!" roared Robbie "look into my eyes. I'm not afraid of you anymore! You killed my grandfather, you tried to kill my friends, you're not gonna kill me!" Robbie raised his hands into the air. Blue sparks started flying again. Rocks and debris whipped around the giant beast, as though he was encased in a prison of swirling stone. Robbie looked up at the beast and for the first time, he truly wasn't afraid. It seemed stunned. **"I believe now, in the scrolls, in myself. All of this happened for a reason, and I believe now!"** The beast began to fall about in a daze. Little slits appeared all over its body, they revealed green light from inside the nightmare. The slits expanded and the creature howled in pain. It clutched its temple as though an incredible headache had just come over it. Suddenly the beast was torn apart from inside, a bright green light shone out, fragments of nightmare scattered everywhere, then dissolved and disappeared. The green light went out. It had been destroyed. Robbie stood triumphant, a smile on his face.

"Gotcha"

"Bravo, bravo!" came a familiar voice from behind. Robbie turned, it was Ziva Vaugier. She stood on the street, her sword drawn. "You're safe!" said Robbie. "Why of course, and it looks as though you do not need my help." "Ziva we've got to tell the Professor,

I can stop them now!" Ziva smiled, you really *are* the one."

BOOM BOOM BOOM

"Wait, Robbie." The sound of nightmares approached. Ziva looked into the sky. The nightmares were coming together. Hundreds of them swarmed the skies and made their way through the streets. They seemed to have a purpose now, to move toward the source, east, to Havisham Hall. "They're not stupid," said Robbie "they know I'm coming for them. They're scared." "They should be," said Ziva "they should be."

Chapter Twenty

THE TEMPORAL CHAMBER

Robbie was full of newfound energy and looked forward to the challenge ahead. He'd finally be able to complete his mission, to complete his granddad's wish. BEEP BEEP, BEEP BEEP

The sound emanated from Ziva's leather jacket. She took out her beeper and checked the screen. She looked disappointed. "What, what is it?" asked Robbie. "You are to return to the Circle, William Humble needs to speak with you."

"Now?"

Ziva nodded, as if to apologise without saying sorry.

"Great, just when things were getting interesting."

Robbie, Sarugril and Alicia had all been summoned to the temporal chamber room. Robbie had seen the signs for it all over the Circle. He knew that temporal meant time, but he didn't know what they used it for. As they walked along the corridor that led there Robbie looked up at the holographic images of Shellon Mace. But instead of feeling afraid Robbie wanted to meet him now, to meet the man that was responsible for so much misery and pain and to stop him, just like his granddad would have done. He was glad he had met Alicia, she made things a little easier. In fact, if it wasn't for her he wasn't sure if he could have gotten this far at all. He glanced over at her and she smiled back. She knew that he was thinking about her. "What does he want Sar?" said Robbie trying to act cool. "Just to discuss our options." "But I know what to do now, I've proven that I can beat them." "Yeah Sar, why don't we just..." Alicia stopped, she knew from Sarugril's expression that he was still mad with her. "Listen to what he says, that is all I ask, if you do not agree then we can try something else, but I do not want there to be unnecessary risks." Sarugril seemed determined in his view. Robbie nodded, simply to get it over and done with. "Which reminds me" started Sarugril again "I am not sure if you are aware, but each human member of the Circle is assigned a bodyguard." Robbie looked to Alicia, she went bright red. "No, I had no idea" he lied." "I was your grandfather's defender Robbie, it would be my honour to become yours also." Robbie was genuinely appreciative. "That means a lot Sar. Thanks." "It is my pleasure."

The sliding doors to the temporal chamber room opened and they entered inside. The temporal chamber sat in the middle. It was a spherical contraption made of stainless steel, there were wires coming from the base of it that slotted into the walls on either side. Plastic tubes came from the back and stretched all the way to the far wall. There were a group of scientists preparing it for testing. There were also plastic partitions set up around the sides, behind those there were control panels to activate the machine. Robbie looked up at the charts and diagrams that were spread throughout the forty-foot space. Inspecting them closely he could tell that they were all related to time travel. On the walls there was a list of dates.

April 15th 1912	Sinking of the Titanic
July 8th 1947	Roswell, New Mexico
Nov 22 1963	Kennedy Assassination

The list came right up to the present day. It was clear that William and his team of scientists often used the machine. William Humble came to join them. "Thank you for coming Robbie, I hope it will be worth your... well, time." "Can you explain what the chamber does?" said Sarugril hurrying him up. "Well, you see, in a way, this is the mother of all portals, the big cheese, the proverbial grandfather of them all, the..."

"William, we understand, can we move it along?"
"Ah, yes, of course, well, here it is, our pride and joy, our temporal chamber." "You want me to trap Lucy in *there*?" said Robbie. "Well, that *is* the general idea, yes." "That's crazy," said Alicia "have you *seen* his sister?" "William, you said this was one big portal?" inquired Robbie. "For all intents and purposes, yes. There's a line running through history, a thread if you like. We have visited all of the places you see here, to carry out business." "We've changed everything" said Alicia. "She's right" said William Humble "behind every event in history there is a bigger story. Take the Titanic for example. Most people think that the Titanic struck an iceberg." "It did" said Robbie. "Be that as it may the reason why has always been kept from the world. The truth is that the ship was hijacked by Nefaru time agents. It took them just ten minutes to secure every deck. We managed to rescue some of the passengers and later went back to destroy evidence

of laser marks and other modern equipment, we also made sure that nobody discovered the remains of the vessel until 1985, but the rest unfortunately is history." "And Roswell?" "Roswell's where we found FAL." A little creature appeared from behind William. It was small, grey, and had black eyes that receded back into its head. He was a portal guardian. The very same one that Robbie had seen the first time that he had come to the Circle. Robbie looked concerned. "What gives you the right to change history?" "We don't change it Robbie, we correct it." "Whatever happened happened to protect many, not just the few. If sacrifices aren't made, everyone dies." Sarugril stepped forward. "There is a line Robbie in the glyph that I showed you. It symbolises blood, but it also symbolises time. That line is a thin thread that keeps us from destruction. Time is fraught with danger. We fight every day to protect it. The human race is weak at certain points in history. Mace knows this. He is constantly trying to attack us through cracks in time, known as time rips. Through these rips his agents can enter. Sometimes people are lost in the battle but we must continue the fight. If we do not Mace will win." Robbie didn't like it, but he understood it. He nodded. "Alright, let's get on with this. What's your plan William?" "Well Robbie the way I see it it's too risky to confront your sister like you did her bodyguard. There's no telling what could happen to her during the separation process. By using the temporal chamber we could send her back in time safely." "No way," complained Alicia "that won't work. Especially after what happened last time." "That won't happen again I assure you," said William. Sarugril interjected "If we get the girl you're sure you can send her back. All of this will stop?" "You know time travel Sarugril the variables are interchangeable. In short, no I can't be sure, but there's always a chance." "Robbie, what do *you* think?" asked Sarugril. "We should try. If it doesn't work we'll do it my way." "Excellent," said

Humble "now, all I need is for you to bring your sister here. After that the temporal chamber will send her back to a timeline before the destruction of the Dream Streamer." "What happens to all of you?" said Robbie. "Well, if everything goes to plan you won't remember any of this, you'll just wake up and it will be like none of this ever happened. It will be just a normal day." "So, I won't have met any of you?" Robbie didn't like this idea. He looked to Alicia. She looked to the floor in disappointment. Everyone fell quiet for a few seconds. The air was heavy. Robbie broke the silence first. "I guess this is one of those sacrifices that you're talking about." "Perhaps it is Robbie," said Humble placing a hand on his shoulder. "Take care of yourself, and good luck out there." Humble left the room. "Rob, you don't have to do this you know, we could find another way" said Alicia. "I hope that's true." "Same here." She looked at him and thought about what it would be like if he went back to the way things had been and she never knew him. She knew she could never find him and tell him the truth, she was sworn to secrecy by the Circle. She knew Robbie was thinking the same thing. "Alright you two let's get ready." Sarugril reached into his utility satchel and clicked his materialiser. "Good luck everyone."

A portal emerged and they went through. They reappeared on London Bridge. Bright blips began to appear on the screen. "She's close." "So let me get this straight," said Alicia "you wanna get so close to her that you attach this materialiser, and send her back through the portal into the temporal chamber?" "Exactly." "Isn't that a little dangerous?" "Warriors do not concern themselves with danger" commented Sarugril. "Robbie, seriously, the last time we tried something like this you ended up in the infirmary." "That's not gonna happen this time." Alicia could see that Robbie was different somehow, the news of Oswald's murder had shaken him, but he was changed, braver, stronger. The blips became clearer. "Prepare yourselves," said Sarugril. Soul reapers began to fill the sky. Their screeching was almost unbearable. Alicia covered her ears and crouched down. Sarugril looked up, and crunched his knuckles as though he was preparing for battle, and Robbie, Robbie just waited for Lucy, calm cool and collected. Robbie could see Lucy at the far end of the bridge, a collection of her nastiest nightmares around her. He walked out in front of Sarugril and Alicia. "I'll take care of Lucy. Sar, you go for the nightmares." "Great," complained Alicia "and me?" "Keep a portal open for us, if we get into trouble we'll need a quick escape." "Got it." Robbie motioned for Sarugril to take the left hand side of the bridge, while he approached from the right. None of the nightmares attacked this time. They were on the defensive. Lucy looked so human, so normal. She'd picked up a red ribbon that looked strange in her hair. Robbie assumed that she'd taken it from one of the destroyed shops in the city. She looked at him so vacantly, as if she was just a shell of a person. Robbie knew that he had to fight her to free her. He had to try and make William's plan work. "I want my sister back!" he shouted to her. "Come and get her!" Robbie took off running. The nightmares bolted forward. Robbie hunkered down into a ball and sent an energy wave that knocked them flying over the sides of the bridge and plunging into the water below. More of them darted for Sarugril, he used his electro whip to subdue them. Soul reapers flew out from behind Lucy and attacked. Robbie tilted his head and looked up at them, as if he wasn't scared at all, just curious. They burst into green balls of light and disappeared. "It's him," whispered Alicia to herself "it's really him." "I don't want to destroy you," called Robbie to the infiltrator "but I will if I have to!" The infiltrator stretched out its arm and motioned for Robbie to come forward. "Have it your way" he took off toward her. Out of the corner of his eye he could see Sarugril running along the railings at the side of the bridge. The 8ft Holocite leaped onto

Lucy and knocked her to the ground. He reached into his utility satchel and placed the materialiser on her. "Prep the gate" he called to Alicia. "Ready to go!" The portal appeared on the bridge. "Robbie, we did it!" shouted Alicia over the rushing wind from the portal. The demon seemed nervous, scared even. It looked up from the ground and for the first time it saw Robbie as a real threat. His belief in himself shone out like a bright light that petrified the beast. "Stay away," it growled "I will destroy you all!" Robbie stepped calmly forward. "You can't do that, I'm stronger than you now. I'm the master of my fear, not you." The beast began to disintegrate, to weaken. "Sar, now!" screamed Alicia. Sarugril hit the materialiser. "No, wait!" shouted Robbie. It was too late. Lucy had been sent back to the Circle, back to the temporal chamber. Robbie looked on and thought of his sister, he followed them inside.

Robbie, Sarugril, Alicia and a barely conscious Lucy returned through the portal and re-emerged in the room. "Quick, get her inside." Sarugril carried her inside the temporal chamber. The door closed on her. Robbie was reminded of the night that she went inside the Dream Streamer, the night that all of this started. The infiltrator suddenly came to life. It kicked and lashed at the door and smashed against it with her head. "She can't get through that thing right?" inquired Alicia. "Absolutely not, those walls are ten inch thick reinforced steel, her abilities will be useless." Robbie looked troubled. "Will she be OK in there?" "You have my word Robbie. Perhaps you and Alicia should take a break, it's not an easy process to watch." Robbie looked at Lucy, put his hand to the glass of the chamber and walked outside. Alicia followed. "You'll regret this" growled Lucy from within the temporal chamber. "I doubt that" replied Sarugril, arms folded in defiance. William Humble paced in panic. "You! Release me at once!" "Don't listen to her William," ordered Sarugril. "Infiltrators always prey on the weak minded." "Ok...

hey!" "You don't believe you can win this war do you?" mocked the infiltrator "You and your pitiful Circle of freaks and weaklings. You entrust your future to a boy you know nothing about." "We know enough." "No, you *believe*." "Belief *is* enough" retorted Sarugril. The infiltrator inhabiting Lucy's body began to laugh. "I cannot wait for his return. I cannot wait for him to destroy this planet. He will begin here, in London, then spread like a virus throughout the world, until every scrap of humanity lies broken, wretched and quivering at his godly feet!"

"Finished? William, light her up."

William nodded and went behind a plastic reinforced partition near the machine. He put on a pair of thick black goggles and grabbed a lever that was in the middle of a control panel. He slowly brought it down until two giant coils at either side of the chamber began to emit a blue glow that even Sarugril looked away from. Slowly, Lucy was blocked out by the coils rays. Then the rumbling began. "What is that?" roared Sarugril over the deafening noise. "It's the sound of time changing direction!" shouted William. The vision was almost beautiful, but horrific at the same time, like the detonation of an atom bomb. This was something that in a perfect world had no place. A whirring sound started up in the machine. "Wait a minute," said William "that's not right." The screen on William's control panel showed time lines opening and closing like doors. "How, how is that possible. The infiltrator" he said to the howling wind.

"You're trying to let him through, aren't you!" William grabbed the lever he used to start up the machine and yanked it back into position. The sound slowly faded and the intense rays fell to a low dim. "William, why did you stop?" "It was too dangerous, the infiltrator was attempting to open a time rip, presumably to allow Mace into our world." "How could we have been so stupid? Is the girl OK?" "She should be fine." "Should be... wait, William, why is she still here?" "According to my readings, she's not." "That's impossible, I'm looking at her." "Oh no" said William bringing a hand to his sweaty forehead. "What is it William, what's happened?" "I believe I've separated the time lines." "Meaning?" "I've sent Lucy into the distant past." "That's good news, isn't it?" "Not quite, it appears that, due to the effects of temporal travel and as a result of her combined DNA with the infiltrator she has, well, aged, dramatically." "You've turned her into an old lady?" "Well, um, yes, precisely." William looked into the temporal chamber and saw Lucy unconscious, he still didn't know if she was the real Lucy, or whether the infiltrator was still with her. The only thing he *did* know was that now there were two Lucy Havishams.

Emily sat outside the mansion on a rickety old wooden bench. Leaves blew about her feet and the wind caught her curly brown hair. She had a grey scarf dragged over her mouth. She didn't want to stay inside the mansion, not anymore. A figure at the end of the garden motioned for her to come forward. "You!" said Emily in disbelief. It was the old woman. Emily didn't know what to say after this, there was nothing *to* say. "You are wondering how I knew, about the machine, about your family." "Are you responsible?" said Emily angrily. "I'd like to think not, though perhaps in a way I am." "What the hell are you talking about? I want the truth. Now!" The old woman let out a cough that turned into three or more violent coughs after that. "You knew Oswald didn't you?" "I knew *of* Oswald yes, though I never met him personally." The old woman coughed again. "You're ill." "Very. Please, Mrs Havisham if you want to know the truth come with me, there isn't much time." The pair moved away from Havisham Hall and walked down the leaf-strewn path. They settled on a park bench just down the road. Emily didn't know what to say at first, she felt threatened by the old woman in a way. She didn't like the fact that she obviously knew more about what was going on than she did. "One of us needs to speak" said the old woman. "Well, there's hardly any point is there, you won't tell me anything about yourself, you walked into my life and told me that my children were in danger, well now they are, in very real danger, are you happy?" "On the contrary Mrs Havisham, I wanted the absolute opposite." "You *knew* this would happen." The old woman nodded. "I tried to warn you, I am sorry, I'm sorry that I couldn't help you further." "Have you come from the Circle, is that how you know these things?" "In a way that's true, yes." "In a way, what does that mean, who the hell are you?" There was silence on Applegate Street but for a few leaves that rustled along the road. "Please," pleaded Emily "I need to know who you are." There was complete silence now. Even the leaves stopped blowing, as if knowing the gravity of the situation. The old woman shed a tear that rolled from her right eye and down her pale wrinkled cheek. She looked at Emily with a sad and vulnerable expression and said "I'm Lucy Mum."

Chapter Twenty One

CLOSE SHAVE

"Lucy... it, it can't be you." Emily went to the old woman's side. The old version of Lucy hung her head in grief. "Look at me, look at me darling." The older Lucy raised her head, slowly, it hurt her now to do so. "It was all my fault Mum, I started all of this." "Lucy, Lucy listen to me, this isn't your fault, none of it, do you hear me. I don't know how this happened but we can fix this." Lucy slowly shook her head. "It's too late for that now. I tried to warn you, about the nightmares, about the Dream Streamer, that's why I came back. I never thought I'd have to live through that night again, but when I saw those creatures, I knew that I'd failed you. I should have listened to Robbie. Where I come from you'd be so proud of him Mum. He does such amazing things." Emily broke into tears. "I'm proud of you both, my beautiful beautiful girl, I'm proud of you both." Emily hugged her daughter tightly and wept bitterly into her hair. "I'm sorry Lucy, I'm so sorry that this happened to you." Lucy smiled a little at this. "I'm not sorry at all Mum, I'm lucky you see, because now I get to live two lives. The one that I've lived in this body and the one that I've yet to live in the other. This body will be gone soon, but Lucy Havisham will still live, in that girl that everyone's fussing and fighting about." Emily smiled faintly. "I'm losing you, aren't I?" The old version of Lucy nodded, and gave her mother a comforting smile. Her old, kind face, scrunched up, but her eyes were bright and fiercely intelligent, behind those eyes she was still a twelve-year-old girl. Lucy was older than her mother now, but she'd always be Emily's little girl. "Nothing lasts forever Mum."

Lucy began to stumble, Emily caught her in her arms. "No... please... I need more time. I need more time with you." "There's still a little girl out there that needs your help" said the older Lucy. This didn't help, to Emily she was still losing a daughter. Lucy looked up at her mother. "Don't you understand Mum, we have the rest of our lives together." Lucy smiled and her eyes gently closed. A faint breath came from her mouth and she died in Emily's arms.

Sarugril stared into the temporal chamber. His eyes fixed on Lucy, strained to pick up a breath, anything. Lucy's face twitched inside the chamber. "She's back," said Sarugril in relief. "Don't get too excited, we still don't know how much of her is Robbie's sister, and how much is Mace's infiltrator." William tapped on the chamber window. "Hello, hello in there." Lucy rose to her feet but kept her eyes closed." Lucy Havisham is that you in there?" The girl had her head hung low so that her features were obscured by her long dark hair. "Open it," ordered Sarugril "I'm going in." "That's not advisable Sarugril, we don't know what we're dealing with here." "Open it." William nodded to a technician and the locks on the temporal chamber were released. Sarugril hunkered down and walked inside. "Humans and their fancy toys," said the infiltrator. It looked out the window of the temporal chamber. "I've been inside a machine like this before. I believe it belonged to your friend, Oswald." "You never knew my friend you scum." "I am sorry that we had to kill him, but you see, he really knew too much, we cannot have any threats against our return, that is why we must kill Robbie too." Sarugril crouched down so that he was eye to eye with the infiltrator. "You're nothing, you're a messenger, a servant. You'll be destroyed, as will Shellon Mace. He can't hide forever, and when he returns Robbie will be strong enough to defeat him." "You know, these machines really are amazing. I've seen the future Holocite, and well, let's just say it is not so bright for your little human friend." "Lies don't work on me." The infiltrator began to chuckle to itself. "Oh not lies my dear Holocite. Reality, I have seen it happen. I've been there. I've been there when the boy dies at my master's feet." Sarugril went to step outside.

"I've heard enough." The moment Sarugril had his back turned on the infiltrator it fired a flameball. Sarugril's back caught on fire and he stumbled away in pain. The infiltrator stepped out of the chamber and lit up in flames. Scientists and technicians went running in panic. "Ha ha, fear, I love it!" The infiltrator fired jets of flame around the room. William Humble crouched down under a desk in the corner. "You there," he called to a young technician "lock down the doors, don't let her escape." "Doors locked" replied the technician. "Wait, sir, someone's overriding the security system. The locks are being released." "But, that's not possible" said Humble. "They're being released by somebody in the higher levels, the signal is coming from a workstation in the Intel Centre." The doors opened and Lucy walked out, free to roam the Circle. Her laughter echoed down the corridors. Up above the temporal chamber and the floors above that, a man sat alone at one of the work panels. He was high up in the pillars that were dotted around the first floor of the Intel Centre. He entered his personnel code into one of the computers and waited. There was a short burst of static and then a face appeared. It was difficult to tell what the strange shape was at first but soon it transformed. Transformed into one of Shellon Mace's vile guards. "Oh, it's you" said the guard. "Yes, it's me. I need to speak to him." "Lord Mace doesn't wish to be disturbed by... your sort." "Listen you ugly little toad, I have information for him, Important information... or should I wait and let him hold you personally responsible." Mace's bodyguard looked bothered. "Hang on." He left the screen. A darkness seemed to cover the camera, the man knew that Mace was near. A lump came in the man's throat. It was as though Mace was freezing him through the screen. "Yeeeessssss" said Mace, as though snakes were speaking for him. "Lord Mace, the girl, Lucy Havisham, she has been captured by the Circle. I have taken steps to ensure her safe exit but it's become clear that the boy is responsible." "This, Robert Havisham? I can see now that he will cause problems. See to it that he suffers the same fate as his grandfather." "That may not be easy, he believes now." "Believes. In that piece of ancient parchment?" "The Holocite has shown him the way Lord Mace." "Then kill *him* too, kill them all! I have unfinished business with Lombardi, I will not be stopped by a human child." "But Lord Mace, he's more than that." "MORE!" roared Mace. "You sound like you admire the little brat, perhaps you have lost your nerve for this mission, or don't you want to see your beloved family again?" "Please, don't hurt them. Are, are they safe?" "Quite" replied Shellon Mace pointing to the holding cells. The man stared into the screen and could see the imprisoned Centaborgs all huddled together, miserable and gasping for air. "Complete your mission and report back." "Yes Lord Mace." The man switched off the computer and turned in his seat. He rose to his feet and clanked his way into the light.

The man was Samuel Barber.

Chapter Twenty Two

CHAOS IN THE CAVES

Sirens rang out on the corridor. "Temporal Chamber compromised. All personnel please rise to the next level." "I knew it!" growled Robbie. Robbie left Alicia's side and darted down the corridor toward the temporal chamber. The smell of burning plastic filled his nostrils. The door was open and smoke came flooding out. "What happened, where is she?" "I'm sorry Robert, it's my fault" said William. "Just tell me where she is!" "I have no idea, but wherever she's gone she had help from inside, the security doors were overridden." "Where are the doors operated from?" "The higher levels. I hate to say it, but whoever let your sister escape had high security clearance." Robbie ran out of the room and made his way to the higher levels. He was furious, because he knew that whoever had set the infiltrator free was also the one who had killed Oswald. He had a clear picture of who that person was now, he just needed to prove it. Deep in his thoughts, Robbie bumped right into Professor Lombardi. "Robbie, I just heard. I never should have entrusted this operation to Humble, I should have listened to you." "Professor that doesn't matter right now, I know who set the infiltrator free, who murdered my granddad." Lombardi looked shocked "You're quite sure of this?" Robbie nodded. "Well I assume you have some evidence against this person?" "That's what I'm on my way to find, can you meet me at the higher levels later?" "Of course" said Lombardi, visibly stunned.

Lombardi met Robbie a few minutes later. Robbie had assembled a group including Alicia, Ziva, Gordon Bryson, Sarugril and Samuel Barber. They were all standing behind a row of computer monitors. "Professaw, this is most irregulaw. May I awsk why you called us here?" "He didn't call you," said Robbie "I did." "You?" said Samuel "But, under what authority?" "The authority someone gets when you murder their grandfather." "Murder? What are you talking about?" "The infiltrator escaped because someone on the higher levels bypassed security protocols in the temporal chamber room." "But, that can't be true, who would do such a thing?" "You would!" snarled Robbie. "I traced the signal back to this computer. We searched the CCTV cameras. You were seen leaving the same computer after the infiltrator had been released from the chamber. It was you, you're the one who put the infiltrator into the Dream Streamer. My granddad would never let you get away with it so you killed him." "You're totally paranoid, all of you. This is a huge mistake, Professaw listen to what he's saying." "I've suspected him for a long time," continued Robbie "when I was brought here on the first day. Samuel knew that my granddad was working on the Dream Streamer, something he never told anyone, not even you Professor." "Well, I certainly didn't know until you told me." "I decrypted the messages that had been deleted in the Hub too, they were all related to the Dream Streamer, when I traced the signal I discovered that they all came from Samuel's office. He deleted them because they could be traced back to him. The one thing he forgot to erase was the memory of the medbot in the infirmary. If I hadn't been attacked by that nightmare and ended up there I'd never have found the truth." "The evidence is irrefutable," said Ziva Vaugier stepping forward "monsieur Barber knew that Oswald's soul echo would contain no mention of a spy among us, therefore it would be safe to bring Robbie to us, as Oswald had wished." "But for what purpose?" asked Lombardi "why do it Samuel?" "To kill the boy" said Sarugril from the corner of the room. "Barber knew that with Robbie out of the way Mace would be free to return to earth unopposed. He did it to free family members which Mace had taken hostage on his first appearance through the portal." Lombardi looked at Samuel and could see the guilt seep from every pore of his body. "We should put him to death professor" said Sarugril. "No" said Alicia blocking his way. "That's not what we do." "It's what I do" replied Sarugril nudging her aside. "Matheson is right," said Lombardi "we are not killers. We do not stoop to that level." "He promised me so many things," said Barber "he told me that I would see my family again, that they hadn't died, he said that if I did this I could go back to them." "And all you had to do was kill Oswald" said Ziva. "It's not that simple Ms Vaugier, my life was in danger, he told me that if I didn't do it the Centaborg race would be eliminated, what choice did I have?" "So you're a killer *and* a coward" said Alicia. "You didn't want to see your family die so you killed mine instead" said Robbie, his temper rising. Barber glared back at him and his back hunched up, like a cat defending itself. His expression changed into a terrifying grimace.

"Then let me put this another way, I saw which way the tide was turning and I made a decision. You all would have done the same." "You're wrong, we'd never side with Mace," said Bryson "he's a world criminal, and a psychopath and he *will* face Circle justice." "Don't you mean human justice" retorted Samuel. "You have a cheek," said Lombardi "after the rights that Oswald attained for you and your people. Can't you see that Mace has poisoned your mind with his lies?" "Oswald wasn't able to stop thousands of our people from being slaughtered by Mace was he?" "And now you side with the very person who carried out those atrocities?" "Don't you understand Professaw, if we side with Mace we can be saved!" "Mace has no conscience, no sympathy, he fooled you Samuel like he fooled so many others." "I'll not be locked up Lombardi!" "You should have thought of that before you murdered our friend." "Too late, you're all too late. Mace will return and he will punish all of you for this!" Samuel stared at Robbie. "When he comes back I will be on the right side, not here, with these creatures." Lombardi shook his head. He knew that Samuel had lost his mind, another casualty in the war. Sarugril crunched his knuckles. "Get him out of here!" Gordon Bryson reached into his back pocket for a pair of electro cuffs. "Samuel Barber I am arresting you for the murder of Oswald Havisham and conspiracy to corrupt the Circle institution. Anything you say can and will be used against you... what am I saying, you're so screwed." Samuel glared at Robbie again, as if his stare alone could kill him. "Make it easy on yourself horse legs, get moving" said Sarugril.

WHAM

Bryson was suddenly knocked back as he went to fasten the cuffs. Samuel darted away from the gathering and ran through a crowd of Holocites, then escaped down the corridor. "He'll never make it to the entrance" shouted Alicia as they set off in pursuit.

"He's not going for the entrance" shouted Robbie. Samuel stopped, turned, reached into his leg and took out a materialiser. He clicked the top button and a swirling blue portal emerged behind him. "It's too late" conceded Alicia. Samuel smiled, walked backwards into the portal and vanished. Robbie and the others stopped. "Don't worry" said Ziva "I've got an, how do you say, ace up my sleeve? I shortened the range of his materialiser, he will only have gotten as far as the caves." "But those caves are gigantic," said Alicia "we'll never find him." Robbie reached into his pocket and took out a tracker." "They don't call you a genius for nothing," said Bryson "now let's get that creep."

Robbie and the others walked out into the caves. "He hasn't gotten far," said Ziva sniffing the air. She didn't need a tracker, her vampire senses were enough. Nothing could be heard in the caves but the grim plonking of water droplets and the occasional flutter of bat wings. "Keep your eyes peeled," said Bryson "he may be loud, but he's not stupid." "That's debateable," said Robbie eyeing the rocky ground. Wet track marks led deeper into the cave. The team walked further along, following the tracks. Robbie checked the beeps from his tracker. Sarugril was ready for a fight and Ziva looked right at home in the darkness and the fluttering of bats. "It's freezing down here" said Alicia rubbing her arms. "Well, I hate to state the obvious here, but it is a cave" commented Bryson. Robbie went out in front, he wasn't going to let his grandfather's killer get away. "We should split up" said Robbie. "Isn't that the part in horror movies when everyone gets picked off one by one?" said Alicia. "This is no movie, and no one's getting picked off," said Sarugril "do as Robbie says." The others walked on but Alicia stayed behind. "You're going after him yourself aren't you?" Robbie nodded "I can't let anyone else get hurt. I have to stop him." Alicia smiled faintly and nodded, then went to join the others. Robbie set out on his own, in his heart he knew that the first place he'd been with Samuel Barber would be the last place they'd be together.

Samuel bounded over rocks and pools of water to make his escape. A single day hadn't gone past that he didn't feel sick with guilt over what he had done. He had betrayed his friend, killed him to see his own family returned safely, he finally realised that the Dark Lord had used him, and that now it was too late to change the past. At the time he felt that it was necessary, cold and calculated, but necessary. Now he was running from the Circle, blood on his hands and no family to comfort him. Mace had ruined him.

Robbie went back through the series of tunnels that led to the entrance. He knew that Samuel would try to get back to his shop.

SCREEG SCREEG SCREEG

The sound echoed around the stone walls. Robbie glanced about to see where it was coming from. He spied the lights from Samuel's robotic legs shining up and down as the Centaborg negotiated the rocky terrain. He hid behind a moss-covered wall and waited. It was cold and damp, droplets of water fell down on to his forehead and rolled down his cheek.

SCREEG SCREEG SCREEG

Robbie peeked out and could see Samuel enter into the chamber. Robbie realised that this was the same place that Samuel had led him across on the way to the entrance. The place with the bridge of stone that dropped off into nothingness at either side. The bridge across the abyss. Samuel bounded past. Robbie waited until he was about the cross the path to the other side. Suddenly Samuel stopped and looked down. He knew the area had been disturbed. "Ziva, is that you? Or Sarugril perhaps, whoever it is you might as well show yourselves." Robbie walked out from behind the wall. "You're coming with me Samuel." Barber smiled to himself. "And what makes you think that?" "You can make this easy or hard Samuel." "Listen to yourself, all grown up. You believe now don't you, you believe that you're the one that the Holocites speak of." Robbie stayed silent but kept his gaze focused. "I really had no choice." "You always have a choice" replied Robbie. Samuel reached for a compartment in his leg. "Don't! Give it up Samuel!" "Then you're leaving me no choice," replied Samuel smartly. Robbie took his gaze from the compartment for a moment. Samuel reached for a laser cutter and fired at Robbie. Robbie ducked and crouched behind a rock. The laser beam cut through the cave de-stabilising everything it touched. Chunks of rock began to smash onto the cave floor and stalactites fell like daggers. The walls shifted and crunched. Samuel focused the beam on the rock that Robbie was crouched behind. Robbie looked around to see what he could use as a weapon. "I'm giving you one last chance Samuel, stop this!" Samuel laughed hysterically, though he didn't know why. Tears rolled from his eyes, he really *had* lost his mind. "I can never stop now!" Samuel's mechanical legs began to stomp the ground. He walked toward the rock that Robbie was behind. Robbie was left with no choice, he stood up and launched a volley of stalactites and rocks at Samuel. They stabbed into him and pelted him. Samuel lost his balance and slipped backwards into the pit. He disappeared from sight. Robbie ran over and looked down. The Centaborg had clung on to the rocks. He held on at the very edge, his finger tips white with the struggle. "Samuel, take my hand!" "And spend my life locked up by humans, like I was before, never, I'll never go back to that!" Samuel's grip began to loosen. Robbie reached down and grabbed him by the wrist. "Let me go boy!" "I can save you!" Samuel's hand slipped again. Robbie tried with all of his strength to keep him up but the weight of Samuel's mechanical legs dragged him down further. "Samuel, come on!" "Promise me one thing young Havisham. Promise me you'll find my family, find them and bring them home." "I promise Samuel." Samuel finally let go and he plummeted into the darkness of the abyss. For a second there was nothing. Then only the crashing of metal could be heard from above. Robbie stared down into the darkness and felt relief, but also a deep sense of failure. Samuel had been a victim like Oswald had been, and it was all because of the Dark Lord, the destroyer of lives. Suddenly Alicia appeared "Robbie I heard something, are you OK, where's Samuel?" "He's gone..." Alicia stayed silent. Robbie walked on ahead of her. "You had no choice Rob." Robbie didn't reply.

Chapter Twenty Three

WEATHER THE STORM

When Robbie and the others returned to the main building they were summoned to an emergency meeting. It was held in the Circle's top secret war room. Robbie went in first. He was greeted by Professor Lombardi. "I've just heard the news," said the Professor sorrowfully "there was nothing that could have been done for Barber." "So I keep hearing," said Robbie and he took a seat. Alicia came in next, then Ziva, then Sarugril. They all looked a little weary.

"Please, everyone sit," began the Professor. "I know that you've all been through a lot. But in the last few minutes we have learned that the nightmares are returning to their birthplace, which as some of you may know, is Applegate Street. We have gotten reports that the residents of Applegate Street are under imminent threat. This may well be our last chance to destroy these aberrations once and for all." Alicia turned to Robbie "Guess who gets the lucky job." "Thank you Ms Matheson" said Lombardi. "On a serious note, I can think of no better person to lead this mission than you Robbie." Robbie sat up in his seat. "I'm honoured Professor, but, I'm not sure anyone would accept my help. They, think I'm..." "What is it?" "Well, weird." "I think the word weird has taken on a whole new meaning in recent days Robbie, besides you must put your personal feelings aside, you've shown me that you can defeat these things. Now it's time to show everyone else." Robbie had mixed feelings, he wanted to do the right thing, but he also knew that his neighbours mistrusted him. "How can I get people to listen to me when they won't even look me in the face." "They don't need to trust you Robbie, they don't even need to like you, but they *must* listen to you." "Professor." "Yes?" "Can I take someone along?" Sarugril stood to his feet. "I'd be proud to join you." "Um, actually Sar, I was gonna ask Alicia." The Professor smiled to himself "Alicia is an excellent choice Robbie. She's your age, human, and... apologies Sarugril, but, not 8ft tall and built like a wrestler." The gathering chuckled a little, then Ziva rose to her feet, stood in front of Robbie and bowed. "I have faith in you Robbie Havisham, make us proud. I know your grandfather would be if he could see you now." Sarugril walked to Robbie and extended his claw. "I told you once that our differences make us strong. Now go out there and show those kids what I meant." "It's not gonna be easy." "I also told you that sometimes you need to weather the storm." "Alright," said Robbie "let's finish this, once and for all."

Chapter Twenty Four

NIGHTMARES ON APPLEGATE STREET

The old grandfather clock in the hallway of Havisham Hall stopped. Everything was deathly quiet in the mansion and all of its five hundred rooms. Peter and Emily stood in the attic, looking down from where the window used to be.

Robbie and Alicia were out on the road. The children gathered around them. The nightmares hovered above like vultures. Alicia stood upon a makeshift stand, addressing the crowd. "Ok everybody, I know you're scared, but whatever comes down that road, you and only you have the power to stop it. If you're strong and believe hard enough they can't hurt you. Do you see that house?" she said pointing to Havisham Hall. "Robbie Havisham lives there, I know some of you think he's strange and weird, but I have something to tell you, I've never stood beside a braver, more kind person than Robbie Havisham in my life, and any one of us would be proud to call him a friend. Now those things are coming down this road whether we like it or not. We have two choices, we can run, or we can stand and face them like we know we can." The crowd exploded into applause.

As if on cue the children formed into lines, like soldiers on an ancient battlefield. They stood and waited while the sounds grew closer. One boy looked into the sky. Delicate white snowflakes began to flit through the air.

Robbie never felt like a leader in his life but he did tonight. He looked around at the gathering and a great pride swept over him. For once he felt like he was part of something, something that mattered. "It's important to believe they can't hurt you!" he called out. Snarling, hissing, scraping their way up Applegate Street, the nightmares approached. Some of the younger children moved backwards and filtered through the crowd. "Hold the line, be brave!" The nightmares were close now. As they lumbered up the street darkness followed. The lights in each of the houses went out one by one.

Robbie squeezed Alicia's hand, she squeezed back. His heart fluttered, not because of the visions coming for them, but because this was the closest he had ever been to her. "Do you think we'll make it through this" she asked. Robbie hesitated. "I don't know."

The nightmares charged, first the night walkers then the clowns. Swarms of soul reapers swooped down upon the crowd.

"Run, run!"

"Nobody move!" called Robbie.

He glanced at Alicia.

"Let's do this!"

The soul reapers flew down, trying to grab children and carry them into the air. Robbie fired a series of energy balls up into the sky. The reapers ducked and weaved, avoiding each shot. One was caught off guard and was hit. It spiralled uncontrollably and crashed onto the road with a crack. A loud cheer went up. Another Reaper came down fast, howling as it swooped.

"Out of the way!"

The crowd parted. It swept down with its giant claws. Robbie stood in the clearing launched another ball and caught the soul reaper right in the chest. It was sent back down Applegate Street and smashed into the fat green stomach of an oncoming Ogre. It fell to the ground and was crunched under the Ogre's giant feet.

RAAAARGH!

"Oh my god, look at the size of that thing!"

"We can't stop it, there's no chance!"

One of the children looked to Robbie.

"We're not able."

"Yes you are! You've just got to believe that you can. I told you. If you're not afraid, he'll just disappear!"

The Ogre beat at its chest, spit flew from its giant toothy mouth. Three children stood at Robbie's side.

"What do we do?"

"Stay close and believe! You've got to believe that it can't hurt you."

The Ogre approached. Some of the children were shaking with fear, but they had to be strong, they had to believe. "Can't hurt us" said one boy. "It's not real" said another. "We can beat you!" echoed the girl beside them. Robbie knew that with their combined effort they could bring down the beast.

"It's not working" said one of the boys. "Shut up John!" said the girl next to him. Robbie turned to the boy. "He's *your* nightmare, isn't he?" "Yeah... and he's getting closer!" "Listen to me, it's not real, it's just something that you made up, and what isn't real can't hurt you can it?" "I guess not." "I want you to look at that thing and know that it's not real. "I'll try."

The Ogre was at least 12 ft tall. It was covered in scars and had two beady blue eyes that darted about like flies. Grown men would have run and hid from such a sight.

"I'm not afraid of... you're not real!"

Suddenly the beast stopped, and brought its giant barrel-like hands to its ears. The nightmare staggered about and swung in pain, knocking a collection of clowns up into the air. They crashed into the sides of houses. One smashed Mrs Oldham's garden gnomes. A smile crept across the boy's face. He was starting to believe.

"It's working, it's really working" said the girl. The Ogre began to split apart. Green cracks emerged in its rough skin. It let out a deafening howl. It stretched and contorted as if something was trying to break through its skin. Then the nightmare exploded into thick leathery chunks. The green smoke inside it drifted skyward. "It worked, it really worked!" "Good job," said Robbie.

"You did it John, you really did it!"

The snow was coming down heavy now. Robbie could hear howls and screams coming from inside the drift. Some children stood defiant, confronting their nightmares, others weren't ready and fell back. Robbie looked on as one girl came face to face with *her* nightmare.

Sally Jones was being pursued by a pack of sleek black rats. They scurried down the road, nipping at her heels. She ran as fast as she could but the rats were relentless, soon she ran out of breath. Sally stood up on two bins by the side of the road. Robbie looked on through the snow. He knew she could do it. She just needed to believe in herself.

"I'm not afraid," she said to herself "I'm not afraid, I'm not afraid." The rats hadn't budged. She thought back to that night when she was a baby. The night that the disgusting black rat had crawled over the blankets of her cot while she lay awake. She gritted her teeth in anger, and said to herself. "I'll never feel like that again!" Sally opened her eyes a little. There were tiny squeeks, but the noises weren't coming closer, they were fading. Some of the rats had vanished, others were scrambling away. Now *they* were the ones who were scared. She stepped down from the bins and chased after them. Sally concentrated harder, really believing the words. Soon the sea of disgusting vermin had become one great big pillar of green smoke. It rose and vanished into the air. She had defeated her nightmare. Sally looked to Robbie and smiled.

Across the street, a boy named James was being backed into a corner by *his* nightmare. *His* nightmare was a hideous and creepy looking clown. It snarled and hissed at him, and clutched a red balloon. James stood staring into its eyes. The clown moved closer, its left claw shot from its sleeve. James didn't flinch. He was brave now, he believed, because he had seen what his friends had done. He saw how they had taken down that Ogre. Still, the nightmare moved closer. Just as it was set to attack, it suddenly vanished. James had beaten it, he had believed.

The more belief that surged through the crowd the weaker the nightmares became. Robbie could feel it in the air, things were changing. The balance of power had shifted. He looked around the street and saw that everyone was confronting their own nightmares, their own demons, things that had kept them awake at night, things that had worried them. Everyone was fighting back.

Gretchen Oldham stepped out of her house and into the battle. Snarls, growls, and hisses froze her bones. She gazed in fear at the thousands of snakes, rats, giant bats and other revolting creations. Among the crowd of nightmares and children she thought she spotted something. It scurried about by people's feet. Oldham stepped back, afraid that it was coming for her. It moved fast, it had four little legs, it was white, and fluffy. "Sniffles! It's you, it's really you!" Sniffles ran across the road and into his owner's arms. "Shnuckems I missed you. Mummy missed you!"

The nightmares retreated from Robbie as he walked along the street. It was as though there was a bright light shining from inside him, a light that only nightmares could see. They hated it. It was courage, bravery, decency, goodness, everything they detested. They knew they couldn't beat him. He was far stronger now than they would ever be, because he was the one that the Holocites had written of, he was their warrior, their hero.

Robbie could sense that Lucy was close by. He charged his right hand. "You cannot win boy!" came her voice from within the snowdrift.

"Come out and fight me you coward!"

"Big words from little Robbie Havisham!"

"Leave now, and I won't have to destroy you!" shouted Robbie.

"How can you destroy me, if you cannot see me!"

"Who says, I can't see you. Dad, now!"

From the attic window Peter tapped into Lucy's mind and found her position among the nightmares. "She's right in front of you son. Go get her, I'll wear down her defences!"

The infiltrator watched as a glowing blue light came through the snow. "How, how did you find me!" "I've got friends in high places, now give up!"

Robbie and the infiltrator stared at each other through the snowstorm. "Let her go, you're beaten." The demon laughed. Robbie fired two energy waves that knocked it onto the Browning's front lawn. Lucy shook the snow off of herself and rose to her feet. Alicia arrived in time to see what was going on.

Robbie raised his hand and was about to fire again. "Robbie, you're hurting me!" It spoke in Lucy's voice. It *was* Lucy. "Robbie, don't stop!" shouted Alicia "it's the infiltrator. It's trying to trick you!" "Rob, help me!" continued the demon. Robbie stood still.

"What if you're wrong?"

"I'm not, quickly, get her!"

"You're killing me," said the infiltrator. The nightmares began to creep back and gather around the fight. Robbie doubted himself. "Human," said the demon "all too human." It took advantage of the situation and fired a ball of flame that shot out over the street scorching trees and burning a row of cars. Robbie leaped above the flames and landed back to earth by kicking the infiltrator back across the garden. It snapped to its feet immediately. "I will never release her. You'll have to kill us both!" Robbie didn't listen. He just concentrated. As he did a protective shield rose around him. The infiltrator fired a jet of flame that just bounced off of the shielding and fizzled out.

"Impossible!"

Robbie looked into Lucy's eyes as though mesmerised. The fighting still went on behind him, but he stood in perfect calm. Emily and Peter looked on from the lab, their hearts in their mouths. "What's he doing, what's happening down there?" "I have no idea," replied Peter in puzzlement. The light that the nightmares could see in Robbie became visible. It shone like a beacon, destroying any nightmare that was too close to him. Robbie's eyes turned white and the shield fell down around him. He didn't need it anymore. The infiltrator stumbled back in fear. "Please, please." Robbie raised Lucy into the air and looked up at her as if she was just a toy. "Robbie, how, how are you doing that?" shouted Alicia. She knew what Robbie could do, but this was different, he was changed somehow. "I want you to send a message to your master. Tell him that when I'm finished here I'm coming for him, tell him he's not safe, wherever he goes, whoever he tries to hurt I'll find him and I'll destroy him." The infiltrator nodded, struggling in the air. "Please, please don't hurt me." "You don't belong here," said Robbie "none of you do." Robbie shut his eyes and blocked out the voice. Peter looked on from the lab window and sent a psychic message to his daughter. "Lucy, can you hear me in there? I'm setting you free now."

The infiltrator slowly began to rise from Lucy's body. It was draped in black rags, like a Soul reaper, but it looked even more menacing, more evil. Its long pale and scrawny arms appeared almost human. Inside the hood of its dark cloak Robbie could make out two demonic red eyes. The infiltrator levitated above like a spirit as it struggled and wriggled and clutched at Lucy's body, trying not to be separated from her. It was impossible, Robbie was too strong.

"NOOOOO!"

The infiltrator was violently extracted and Lucy's body fell exhausted to the ground. Alicia ran to her side. The infiltrator growled and snatched as it hovered overhead, like a wicked dog let loose from its leash.

"Mace will destroy you boy, you have no idea of what lies ahead!"

"I'm ready for it."

"This was a test, only a test. You are a boy, he is the Dark Lord! There can only be one outcome. YOU WILL DIE!"

"You first!"

Robbie flung one final shockwave at the beast. It blasted apart with the impact and a bright white light was sent out over Applegate Street. The noise of the explosion shattered all of the windows in each of the houses. Gretchen Oldham cowered in fright. The sky was lit up like a firework. The crowd of children burst into applause and cheered into the night.

No one on Applegate Street feared their nightmares after that. They didn't fear what wasn't real. Robbie looked down the street at the children that were cheering him on. They had all but destroyed the army of nightmares. He ran over to Lucy. "She's not coming out of it" said Alicia. "Luce. It's Robbie, wake up." She didn't respond...everything was quiet now but for the last of the nightmares being dispatched. "Rob, is she?" Lucy shot up from the grass.

"Luce, is it you?"

"No, it's Darth Vader, of course it's me!"

"Smart, snappy, arrogant, yep, it's Lucy alright."

"Well it took you long enough! That thing was starting to drive me crazy. Being possessed isn't everything it's cracked up to be ya know."

"Hi. I'm Alicia."

"Oh. Hey. Um, sorry for trying to kill you by the way."

"Yeah, I'm getting that a lot lately."

Lucy turned to Robbie. "Well then, my little brother finally stopped being a wuss. Doesn't mean I'm gonna stop making fun of you though." "I knew you'd say that. Come on, let's go home."

Emily and Peter stood in the attic and watched as they returned to the mansion. "He's done it. He's really done it!" shouted Emily. She looked down at the children and at the damage that had been caused to the street. "Em, Peter darling, how exactly do we explain all of this? I mean, it's not like people are going to forget." "Let's just say I can be very persuasive," said Peter tapping the side of his head. "Peter, you wouldn't!"

Chapter Twenty Five

GREAT EXPECTATIONS

That night the Havishams had a gigantic feast. Alicia was invited of course. Emily arranged everything to perfection, she took out her best cutlery and the entire dining hall was covered in candles. Everyone sat at a long pine table and they ate Turkey with Cranberry sauce, spiced pork, and glazed ham. For dessert they had ice cream with chocolate sauce and sherry trifle. After stuffing themselves with more than enough food, Robbie, Lucy, and Alicia investigated the rest of Havisham Hall, or as much as they could. Alicia was fascinated by seeing old photographs of Oswald and discovering the plans and schematics for his inventions. The place she wanted to see most was Oswald's lab.

On the way up to the attic Robbie passed a portrait of Oswald and suddenly remembered something very important. "Em, I'll be up in a minute," he said to Lucy and Alicia. Lucy raised her eyes to heaven. "Come on Alicia, I'll show you this place, since Robbie's too wuss." Lucy smiled back, as if she didn't really mean it. Robbie laughed it off and walked down the hall to Oswald's room. He sat at Oswald's writing desk and opened his soul echo. The soul echoes pages flicked to the very end. The pages shimmered, Oswald appeared. "Well well, there you are." "Granddad, I did it." Oswald's artificial eyes welled up with emotion. "I always knew you would. I've always known *you* were the one Robert, ever since you were a boy." "But, we, we never saw each other." "Not true. You were just a baby really, your father brought you to the Circle, many years ago." Robbie couldn't believe what he was hearing. "After running some tests I discovered that you weren't like the rest of us, you were, something more. I kept you secret from the rest of the Circle. Although I couldn't prove it at the time, I had suspicions that there was a spy in the HQ." "Barber" whispered Robbie. "It was too dangerous to contact you directly, if anyone had gotten their hands on you the tables could have turned in Mace's favour, we could have lost the war. We needed our secret weapon, our secret weapon is you." "So, what do I do?" "You train, you learn. Listen to Sarugril, he is the best defender in the Circle. Hone your abilities, keep your friends close to you, you will fight many battles together. People will be hurt, some may even die, but without the struggle, without the sacrifice, the world will fall into darkness and Mace will destroy everything." Robbie could hear someone approach. He could tell by the silhouette dancing across the ceiling that it was Alicia. "Rob come on, we're waiting for you." "I thought Lucy was bringing you up?" Alicia began to chuckle slightly. "Between you and me, I think she's a bit freaked out." "It looks as though you've got a date to keep," said Oswald from the soul echo. "Wait, granddad. There's one thing you never told me." "Oh?" "You never told me what *your* ability was." "My ability was knowing. You see, I always knew you were the one. I could see your future. I saw all of the amazing things you would achieve, the friends you would make, the adventures you would have, this was *my* ability." "You knew all of this was going to happen." "It's never about the ending Robert, it's about the journey." Oswald gave a gentle smile and the book slowly closed in Robbie's hands. Robbie knew that he'd see him again soon. Alicia entered the room. "Rob, come on."

Beep Beep. Beep Beep.

Alicia took out her beeper and read the screen. A smile crept across her face. "Lombardi and the others send their regards, between you and me you're officially part of the gang." "I can't wait to see Sar's face when I get back. He'll probably keep going on about how you're such a great warrior, blah blah blah." "You're